Messenger Twelve

James Lynn Bartz

THE WESTBOUND STAGE®

2000

"MESSENGER TWELVE"
First Edition

Copyrighted, © 2000, by James Lynn Bartz

Library of Congress Catalog Card Number: 00-090248

ISBN 0-9678756-0-9

Messenger's Edition: Hard Exterior with Gold-Dust Jacket

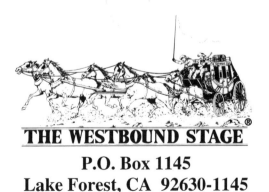

THE WESTBOUND STAGE
P.O. Box 1145
Lake Forest, CA 92630-1145

Printed in the U.S.A.

ACKNOWLEDGEMENTS:

Dr. Robert J. Chandler, Sr. Historian, Wells Fargo® Bank Historical Services, for holding tight reins on a period story that rolls on at unbridled historical gallop;

Marcus De Chevrieux, Curator, Newport Harbor Nautical Museum, for teaching me to cast off, climb the ratlines, unfurl the sails, and set the sails of tall ships without sinking them;

Dr. Charles J. Bellitti, Newport Orthopedics, for assisting me in probing for and removing a lead ball, stopping the bleeding, and patching Reef up without killing him;

Keith J. Atkinson, Director of Public Affairs, Church of Jesus Christ of Latter-Day Saints, for assuring me that the Trowbridges will eagerly defy the Fugitive Slave Act on behalf of a sing-song girl;

Yao Moon-Pin, **Mary Chen**, and **Sherry Cheng**, for consulting with me in Irvine and Newport Beach, California, regarding the nuances of Chinese names and customs;

Judith L. Darnell, Librarian, and **Michael J. Burns, J.D.**, Senior Associate of Seyfarth, Shaw, Fairweather & Geraldson, for researching the law of the California gold-rush era;

Irving Cooper, Screenwriter, for mentoring, insisting upon those endless rewrites, and reminding me frequently that this is Reef's story, Reef's story, Reef's story;

Jeff Millet, Graphic: Publishers, for patience, superb editing, and professional advice, especially regarding firearms and runny noses; and

Beverly Smith and **Carrie Hefte, Esq.**, Wells Fargo® Bank, for gentle oversight and generous support.

Messenger Twelve

"*Go ahead, Atherton. Pick a pretty one.*"

"Ahoy, the longboats."
"Aye. What say you?"
"Stand by to come aboard."
"Aye. Coming aboard."
The oarsmen in the longboats allowed the lines to loosen and waited for the ship to overtake them. Young Reef Atherton was eager to climb aboard the *Polar Star*. He and his mates had rowed for four hours almost without stopping, towing the ship across the glassy surface of the water, fighting to escape the doldrums, and searching for the slightest trade wind. Not one of the parched sails had caught a hint of a breeze.

The heat of an equatorial sun beat down upon them with an incessant fire. Despite the heat and the fatigue, the men stirred with energy and excitement. They joked and laughed about the entertainment that awaited them. Now that their watch had ended, the *pinning* was about to begin. For such entertainment, Reef had little interest and no stomach.

"I'll be the first to pin one," boasted a sailor.

"You corner and trip her for me. I'll do the pinning," laughed another.

"Pin all you want. Then belay, stand aside, and watch the master go to work on this *virgin night.*"

The men booed and laughed. They loved a good virgin night. Virgin night was a misnomer, one that was borrowed from the brothels ashore. No virgins remained among the girls in chains below the decks, and the sun was still high in the afternoon sky. Preparations were under way regardless, and the laughter and joking increased in volume as the replacements took their turn in the longboats.

Reef took his cue and started up the ratlines to the topgallant yard above. He had no desire to witness the debauchery or to endure the goading of his shipmates to participate. He was too young to appreciate the lust that others seemed to have for a helpless Negress.

"Ho, Atherton, what's your hurry?" asked the Second Mate, displaying his authority, his bilge breath, and his tobacco-stained grin.

The first girl was brought up on deck. She was stripped and swabbed front and back with a mop from a lard bucket to the rhythm of the chanting sailors. Reef saw this and begged his leave.

"The new halyards on the main topgallant need serving, sir, or they'll be chaffing through by morning."

Again, Reef started up the ratlines, but the mate intercepted him and pointed to the activity. Two more girls were brought up, stripped, and swabbed.

The three slaves huddled together, crying, and facing each other.

"Stay and play, boy. Show us your skill at cornering and pinning."

"Please, sir, I'd rather not, thank you."

"Ain't it time you became a man, boy?"

Three more girls joined the huddle.

"Please, sir, may I go now?"

The mate grinned. He was enjoying the moment, the boy's embarrassment, and his position of authority.

"Then pick five for us boy, and we'll spare one. You'll be doing the girl a favor. You do want to save one, don't you, boy?"

The oarsmen formed a circle and stripped, after which other shipmates restrained their hands behind them and hobbled their ankles with cords and short lengths of line.

"Tie them tight, mates. Let's play fair," barked the mate.

"Go ahead, Atherton. Pick a pretty one. Save her."

Reef heard the tone of authority in the mate's voice. He knew well the sound of a direct order. He saw no way out, but the glistening black bodies offered him no guidance in making a choice. He remained silent. The mate escorted him to the huddle, pushed aside two of the girls, and realigned them to let Reef peer into their faces. The tone in his voice was unmistakable.

"Pick one, Atherton."

Only one girl caught his eye, his attention, and his interest. She was comely, as young as himself, and her expression bore no tears. No pleas like the others. No supplications. No prayers. Only fear filled her flashing brown eyes. Simple fear. If he could save one, he would save her.

"This one."

The men cheered and the mate released him. Unaware of the crew's intentions, Reef had played the first part of their two-part game. The girl was returned below deck as promised and Reef was satisfied that he had carried out his order. He climbed into the rigging and did not look back to watch the activity on deck.

The first of the remaining five girls was thrust into the middle of the circle. The men began to close upon her amidst the cheering and laughing. By bumping, maneuvering, trapping, kneeling, and crowding, they forced her to the deck.

Two or three sailors pinned her limbs, while others vied to be the first to ravish her. When the first jack succeeded, the spectators cheered and released an additional girl to them and the cycle was repeated until all five girls had spent the energy of all the oarsmen.

Reef was high on the yardarm and lost in his daydreams. Daydreams of becoming a mate, and then a captain, of barking commands, of watching his crew go aloft into the rigging, or work along the polished decks of his own ship.

The sails and rigging of the *Polar Star* would be among the finest on the seven seas if he could have his way. He would be the captain and sole owner of the *Polar Star*, he dreamed, and he would brook none of the nonsense unfolding on the decks below him.

Silence and tranquility eventually returned to the *Polar Star*. Only the sound of the longboat's oars interrupted the stillness, and the sun was setting as Reef lowered himself onto the deck. In Reef's estimation, the men had resumed their normal activities, but in truth they were busying themselves, biding their time, and waiting for him.

When his feet hit the deck, five men were upon him. He fought them as best he could. He did not scream for help, from his father, or from anyone. The men stripped him and lashed him to a larded black body. The girl that he had saved had been bathed, combed, and perfumed for him.

A series of moves by his captors prepared him for his initiation. The girl's arms were tied at the elbows behind his head. Her knees were tied behind his thighs. His arms were tied behind her and the two were deposited into a waiting larded skysail. Without a pause, they were caught up in a series of rolls and pitches, amidst the laughter of the gathering audience. Cheers broke out as the cook passed around the daily ration of grog, and the men rolled, pitched, and tossed the couple in Reef's *maiden voyage.*

Reef was frozen with terror. He had never been close to a free girl before, much less a slave. Her cries and her screams with each toss made him feel her warmth and sense her presence. Her aroma was sweet, her breath was inviting, and his body began to respond to her.

His natural young desire soon mastered his fears, and he surrendered, allowing her nearness and the force of the skysail in full hoist to bring him against her with great force again and again. He soon reached his peak, and he reveled in the feeling of his full manhood.

At the zenith of the sail's arch, the two bodies separated enough for Reef to advantage his position, and he abandoned his innocence within the succeeding half dozen tosses.

Unwilling to allow Reef to enjoy his pinnacle and his captive, and spiriting for additional sport, the sailors' third toss of a "Hip, hip, hooray!" launched the couple high into the air, over the railing, and into the still water below. All hands rushed to the railing, shouting, cheering, and laughing.

Reef was flushed with the chill of the water and the reality of the joke that had been played upon him. The men would consider him a boy no longer. He had passed the test. He disengaged himself from the girl, helped her to the side of the ship, and into the waiting longboat that had pulled up alongside.

"August 15, 1828 ... young Atherton was tried by his shipmates in the performance of his duties. He conducted himself with considerable precision and unflinching intrepidity. The men applauded his resolve, and count him proudly among their numbers."

Amos Atherton, Captain
Logbook of the Polar Star

"... *And may God have mercy upon his soul.*"

In 1832, the writings William Lloyd Garrison's *Liberator* called upon abolitionists to escalate their efforts to free the slaves. In many nations the lawmakers, shippers, and landowners were being harangued to curtail the traffic, and mete out severe penalties including death for those who would place one person into bondage against his will.

Among the abolitionists were the zealots. They were young. Impatient. They wanted action. Now. If results were not forthcoming, they were willing and able to take the necessary measures to produce them. If you stand in the way, you die.

Amos Atherton had the misfortune to stand in their way. In an altercation outside an inn in New Orleans, unidentified members of the Committee of Freemen assassinated him. There were no witnesses. No man was indicted and no man was prosecuted.

Nineteen year-old Reef Atherton attended the burial with three of his shipmates and two of his father's partners. Reef had grown up on his father's ship after his mother died, and the *Polar Star* had been his home, the only home he knew.

Amos had been his father, his mentor, and his friend. As his shipmates lowered the casket into the muddy grave, Reef wept. He was alone in his sorrow.

Reef was the sole survivor of the Atherton holdings, which consisted of bank accounts in New Orleans and London, about $12,000 each, a twenty percent stake in a ship, *Polar Star*, and a ten percent stake in a brig, *Sea Wind*.

Heated arguments erupted among the partners about the future of the ships and revenues.

"I don't like being at the mercy of the 'abs.' Those fanatics are crazy and I want out."

"Let's be calm. We can convert the ship to commercial cargoes and still make money."

"Not as much as we can bringing in slaves. We'll bring them to Cuba."

"No. If we're caught, the ships will be sunk by the warships and we'll all be hanged."

"Nonsense. We can bribe the Cubans. Bring in the slaves at night. Move them overland into the compounds."

"What good does that do? They don't have papers."

"We can pay to get papers. Once they're registered, we can load them aboard ships and transfer them to New Orleans. There's no law against transferring slaves."

The partners paid no attention to Reef, and they did not ask his opinion, although he now owned a larger percentage of *Polar Star* than some of those present. Regardless, he had little interest in the future, and was content to remain silent in his grief.

The partners decided to continue the business, to promote the first mate of the *Polar Star* to captain, and move the trade to Cuba. In Haiti, they could bring the slaves to land under cover of darkness, unload them, and register them as "native slaves" for export at the quartering compounds and transportation yards.

Exporting slaves from Cuba to the Americas was still legal. Importing slaves into Cuba was a crime, but nights were dark, lagoons were plentiful, and witnesses were easily bribed.

At nineteen years of age, Reef Atherton was appointed Bosun's Mate by the new captain of the *Polar Star*. His shipboard performance was outstanding. The *Polar Star* boasted of the stoutest and finest rigging of any ship plying the waves between the Americas and Africa. He was appointed to Second Mate the following year, then to First Mate, and finally, captain by the time he was twenty-five.

Reef was a sterling seaman. He knew his stars and he knew his sunlines. He had paid his men for their loyalties to him, and he had punished them for their betrayals. He had secured the cargoes and he had delivered them. He had ignored the stench, the suffering, the puking, and the wailing of the blacks beneath his decks. Indeed, Reef was a sterling seaman, and he was a master slaver.

He had participated in, then stood by and watched the virgin nights and the maiden voyages. He had become wealthy. He had become respected. For what? He had no one with whom to share his pleasures. He was a lonely man. And no one cared.

"May 12, 1842 ... An undivided one hundred percent interest in fee of the ship Polar Star is conveyed to Reef Atherton of New Orleans ...

An undivided one hundred percent interest in fee of the brig Sea Wind is conveyed to Reef Atherton of New Orleans."

Division Order, U.S. Circuit Court
New Orleans, Louisiana

"*I will serve you for life.*"

Reef Atherton was born of a French aristocrat's daughter. He learned the arts and sciences from his mother. Upon her death, he became a cabin boy on his father's ship at eight years of age, and learned how to survive and prosper in the world about him.

Half a world away, Lin Thai-Saing was born of a prostitute in a slum alley near the wharves of Hong Kong. He knew nothing of life other than scratching for survival from the first moment of his existence to the last. If his feelings for his mother could be called love, then he loved his mother, and no one else.

His boyhood was spent procuring Italian and Portuguese sailors and merchants for her, and stealing food and clothing for her from farmers in the marketplace. He was an avid student of both schools, learning the customs and dialects of his own people in the marketplace, and those of the joking and swearing sailors as they awaited their turn with his mother.

Before he was twelve, he had concluded that only two things in his life mattered: Gold and girls. When he was fifteen, he bought his first girl, a peddler's half-starved twelve year-old daughter, for the equivalent of three American dollars in gold.

She was not by any measure attractive, but he could feed her and put her to work the same day. Besides, he did not have the money to pay forty dollars or more for a *blossom*. Three more years passed before he could sell the first girl and buy his first blossom. By the time he was twenty-three, he was working three blossoms.

In addition to keeping his mother employed, Thai-Saing found that he could work the girls with little effort. A good scrubbing and a dress stolen from the marketplace were all that it took to entice *"ay paisanos"* into his mother's squalid hovel, where the men could pursue their *amo* of choice, and pay for service or for chicken, rice, and wine. Either way, he could practice his Italian grammar with the waiting customers.

He had learned the value of a pretty face, pleasing fashions, and alluring manners. His blossoms already had the first, he could provide the second, but they demonstrated a total lack of grace and gentle manners. He kept the three in sight as they worked each ship arriving at the docks. With his tutelage, at least, they were becoming adept at enticing their own customers, and bringing them to him for approval and payment.

Procuring was one thing, but his duty had become one of administration and management, a task for which he was ill suited. Their quarters were cramped, with little or no privacy, something that the sailors seemed to demand. Their cribs were dirty, but not one of them cared about cleaning themselves, their beds, clothes, or otherwise.

His mother resented the presence of the three young girls, and the four bickered over each trivial jealousy or slight. They had no education, no refinement, and precious little desire to acquire any skills that could enhance and expand the business.

Thai-Saing's sluggishness in responding to his domestic and logistic problems gave incentive to his mother to leave them and take up solitary quarters. That show of independence contributed to her death. She was found strangled in her filthy crib, the victim of two drunken Italian merchants that she had served.

Thai-Saing sank into a fit of deep depression, which almost cost him the rest of his business. Only his plan to avenge his mother brought him back into the daylight.

Bribing a dock officer, he borrowed a uniform and posted semi-official handbills along the docks, in the brothels, and at the gangplanks of each Portuguese and Italian ship. The posters announced that a reward in gold had gone unclaimed for an unidentified citizen's arrest and summary execution of a wanted murderess.

His mother was named as the criminal, and the unknown executioner was proclaimed to be a responsible and civic-minded foreign visitor, and a hero who had shied away from taking the credit and reward that was currently due and payable.

Months passed. Thai-Saing continued to distribute the handbills. To add to Thai-Saing's good fortune, the Italians returned to Hong Kong, learned about the reward, took the bait, and presented themselves to claim it.

"You are the dock officer, Thai-Saing?" one asked.

"Yes."

"We have come to claim this reward," proposed the other.

"Prove to me that you deserve it. Identify her and the circumstances of this legal execution."

They did. Thai-Saing knew by their answers that they were the ones responsible for his mother's death. He bowed, congratulated them, expressed his official words of thanks, and led them to a deserted customs warehouse. He bowed, retrieved the gold from his purse, and paid them in small gold coins. While they were counting it, he clubbed them and spiked them with a boarding pike. While they bled, he tied them, gagged them, and retrieved his gold.

The sound of sobbing reached Thai-Saing's ears. He turned to see a strong boy, about fifteen years old. Wu, a porter and beggar along the docks, had witnessed the murders. The boy opened his arms in supplication, continued to cry, and sank to his knees. Thai-Saing walked over to him.

"Wu. You saw?"

"Yes."

"These Italians. They were friends of yours?"

"No."

"Then, why do you cry?"

"I know of your painful struggle to avenge your mother. My mother also was murdered. Long ago. I was helpless to prevent it. Unable to avenge it. I cry to release my guilt. I cry in joy for you. You have set me free from my bondage. My gratitude has no bounds. Grant that I may serve you always. I will serve you for life."

Thai-Saing raised the pike. He should not let a witness live. He did need help, though, someone to manage and protect his girls while he built his fledgling business. The boy did not flinch or cower before the pike. A sign of great courage. Thai-Saing lowered the weapon.

"Then, you will take my name. Your name is now Lin Wu."

"I am honored to bear your name."

"Help me. Quickly."

They weighted the bodies, dragged them outside into the darkness, and lowered them into the muddy waters of the harbor. Wu was the only witness to the carnage.

> *"March 5, 1843 ... loyalty and service for life, given by hand and by seal to the honorable Lin Thai-Saing."*
> *Lin Wu*
> *Bond Of Indenture*

"This is our moment, and you belong to me."

"Robin. A beautiful little bird with a lovely song. The first to come into your heart, and the last to leave. Will you sing a lovely song for me, my pretty little bird?"

Robin laughed. She delighted in an original poetic overture delivered by a hungry suitor. This opening was better than most. So was the suitor. She thought for a moment and responded.

"Reef. Born a tiny and soft sea animal. But he grows quickly, and stands fast, rock hard, against the waves. Are you standing fast for me, my rock-hard coral Reef?"

She laughed again, mocking him, and enjoying her own spontaneity and her sport at his expense. His response was unexpected, unlike that of her usual red-faced, smiling, and supplicating swain *du jour*.

His silent answer was an unfaltering "rock-hard" stance, a lighthouse "standing fast" against her wave of humor, with the beacons in his eyes sweeping her with his full intensity and lust. His hands took hers and pinned them against the tree.

Indeed. She was Robin Larimore. The Larimores of Beacon Hill. The daughter of Charles Larimore, the principal partner of Larimore Bank. Who in hell does this Romeo think he is? She would not be cowered by his company.

She met his expression with equal intensity, moistening and parting her lips, daring him to proceed any further, and compelling him to remain within the bounds of propriety. After all, they were only one tree and twenty paces away from the picnic tents, and one tree and twenty would not shield them from the gossip that was already whirring along the Common.

To hell with propriety. Reef released her hands, pulled her to him, and encircled her waist with his right arm. In concert with her wide-eyed glare and silent "No!" escaping from her lips, he brought his mouth close to hers before she broke off the intended merger.

"Mr. Atherton, don't you dare. Someone will see. They'll gossip."

To hell with gossip, and decorum be damned. In his arms panted a highborn girl of twenty-three who bordered on God-kneeling perfection. So quite new for him to be in the presence of such an exquisite creature, much less hold her in his arms. So different from the squalor, the screams, and the stench of the black girls chained between the decks of the *Polar Star*.

With milk-white complexion, a waist lost in a single encircling arm, and abundant breasts that pressed hard against him, she had captured him in their first skirmish and he intended to make his surrender unconditional. He had found his Helen of Troy, and it was time to launch the first of a thousand ships.

"Let them babble. This is our moment, and you belong to me."

He forced their kiss, basking in the aroma of her perfume and the taste of her tongue. With his own dark eyes, he met hers, peering at them, marveling at their beauty, depth, and unique myriad patterns. She was beginning to return his kiss when he parted from her.

"And I belong to you."

He kissed her again. Capturing him in her arms, she responded with a mounting fervor and enthusiasm. *Bonjour* to propriety and farewell to spinsterhood. Let the tattlers have their day. She was ecstatic. She had coaxed her childhood puppy-lover, Paul Duchard, to tell her about this rough-cut diamond and to introduce them. She had attracted Reef that instant, lured him away from a wallflower on a pretext, and tested his reaction to her and his resolve to possess her.

She had not found him wanting on any count and she was flushed with her own excitement.

Damn him. Her body was responding with liquid fire, and her soul was filled with the grace of spiritual rapture. She sensed that she needed to come up with a plan. Quickly. Here was a jewel that could use a good cut and polish. Honed by her own hand, and mentored by her father, Reef Atherton would make one damn fine banker.

Reef parted from her with great reluctance, unembarrassed, and unapologetic for their brief and thrilling public union. She pretended to be angry and embarrassed, but surrendered her hand to his waiting arm as they returned to the picnic.

"June 14, 1844 ... he is crude. Crude, demanding, and impertinent. I loathe him, and I will refuse to see him should he come calling."

> *Robin Larimore*
> *Letter to Sarah Carswell*

"... God Himself kneeled and adored you ..."

The parson and witnesses withdrew from the bride and groom, leaving them alone in the sanctuary of the Old North Church. With friends and relatives in attendance, a customary silence intruded upon the ceremony. At this moment, they would speak to each other as man and wife for the first time.

In a few moments, they could address and kiss the members of the congregation and be addressed and kissed in return, but this unique and sacred moment was theirs alone.

No intrusion was allowed upon this time-honored tradition. No enlightenment of their intimate whispers would ever be asked, and none would ever be revealed. Their covenant with each other and their God was the seal that would encapsulate and protect their union forever.

Reef took her hands and looked into her eyes. He spoke with uncharacteristic hesitation, struggling to find the words to express what was in his heart, but coming up with only those that could express his feelings.

"I don't like being here."

"I know."

"You don't know anything about me. About my past."

"Forget the past, my darling. Tell me. What is in your heart?"

"You know how I feel about you."

"Tell me, my love. Here. Now."

"Robin Larimore. Atherton. So delicate. So gentle. I am so unworthy to claim you for my own. Yet, you lend fire to my very soul. When He created you, God Himself kneeled and adored you, as I adore you now."

She was shaken by his blasphemy, even though she knew that he was a godless man. She was stunned by his, what was it, a prayer? She had never heard anything quite like it before. His affirmation was worth testing. Reef waited for her to speak, and she responded with a steady voice.

"Reef Atherton. Today and forever, you are my husband. I am your wife. By your own will, and by your vows, you have created me so. Therefore, this day, you are my God. If your words are from your heart. If they are truly spoken. Then kneel before me. Kneel and adore me, my God. Now."

Seeing the steady gaze in her eyes, and no smile upon her lips, Reef knew that she was serious, but neither had he spoken idly. With a deliberate and steady movement, he descended to his knees in front of her as a uniform gasp flooded the church. He kissed the palm of each hand, looked up at her, and intoned.

"From my heart and truly spoken, I adore you."

Robin's gaze remained fixed upon him. He had passed the test, and again, it was her turn. The murmuring grew louder, but she remained oblivious to all but her husband. She took his hands, placed them upon her waist, looked into his brown eyes, and granted to him her body and her soul.

"Be you my God, Reef Atherton, or my Satan, I impart my immortal soul into your company, and convey my body unto your property. I will be one with you forever."

She took his head in her hands, bent down, and kissed him. The murmuring turned into shocked silence. Such behavior was never allowed in the church, much less in the sanctuary. The parson was dumbfounded and motionless, but any potential protest became moot once the couple arose, clasped hands, and turned to walk down the aisle, through the doors, and out into the brilliant sunlight.

Reef was glad that the tradition of secrecy was followed with religious tenacity. Had their impiety been revealed, their social circle and the Puritanical nobility would have made their life unpleasant, with constant warnings that their so-called sin would not go unpunished.

Murmurs and gossip among Boston's elite had already jeopardized this union. Reef suspected that the Carswells, the lifelong friends of the Larimores, did not approve of the incomparable Robin marrying a common seaman, sole owner of four ships notwithstanding. Reef did not need any religious backlash to boot. He could almost foresee the proclamations of the righteous zealots.

"God will condemn this infidel that leads His young and pure souls astray."

"Destroy this unholy union."

"Entreat these transgressors to repent of their sin."

No matter, thought Reef. Simply by marrying, he felt, there would be ample opportunities for repentance, but he doubted that he would ever be so inclined. He would do anything to keep this one, whether it meant forging an alliance, or even facing an altercation with her God. Or with Lucifer. Or, for that matter, anyone in between.

Anyway, he had no time for such foolishness. His immediate goal was to bed her again and again that night, and to consume whatever lingering innocence she had saved for a husband. After that, he was curious about what she did with her mahogany tresses at night. How does she keep from getting all gnarled up in them during and after a night of sensual indulgence?

Despite Paul's persistent and determined efforts at breaching her virtue over the years, Robin had saved everything for her wedding night. This was her secret gift to her husband, one that she was not about to reveal. Why give him the satisfaction of knowing that she was chaste? Keeping him guessing about it was better, lest he boast about claiming the prize to his friends and using it to his advantage.

She had other things on her mind. She would find a way to make him play out her fantasy with her. She would call it *Revelations*, a game that would make him bare his soul to her and enable her to reveal some titillating wedding-night details to her girlfriends. They would be so envious of her, the first of her close circle to marry.

To get Reef to reveal his feelings, she would present her feminine fruit to him one taste at a time, slow his advances, and make him account to her aloud just how much he was enjoying its consumption.

"January 30, 1845 ... Captain Reef Atherton, formerly of New Orleans, and Miss Robin Larimore of Beacon Hill, exchanged vows of matrimony in the presence of her family and friends."
The Boston Liberator

" ... I will prepare you to receive your husband."

Reef Atherton had been most fortunate in meeting and courting the unique and elegant Robin Larimore. Lin Thai-Saing also tasted the bounty of good fortune the evening that he discovered Shu-Chuan.

Harvests had been meager in the Canton Province following the drought of 1848. Starving farmers were rumored to be selling their daughters for as little as three dollars in gold. Lin Thai-Saing reasoned that girls at that price would be well worth the expense of a journey. He left Lin Wu in charge of his three blossoms, hired a horse, and rode along the Pearl River toward Canton and beyond.

On the following day, he encountered a caravan traveling in the same direction. He rode behind it at a distance, close enough to avoid being harassed by any bandits and far enough to avoid paying the fee to the guide. As the sun was setting, he noticed that the last wagon in the caravan separated itself and took a low road into the rushes alongside the river. No one in the caravan seemed to notice or care.

Thai-Saing stopped and viewed the opportunity that was unfolding. The wagon had no protection away from the caravan. He watched the wagon disappear from view of the caravan. He watched the caravan. He followed the wagon into the rushes for about forty feet and stopped. He dismounted, hobbled his horse, and cut branches to form a makeshift broom. He wiped out all of the wagon's tracks and those of his horse to conceal their path from any bandits who might be following the caravan. He untied his horse and proceeded toward the distant wagon.

He began chanting, walking, and leading his horse toward the direction of the campsite. The reason for the departure of the wagon from the caravan soon became apparent. A foolish young groom was seeking some privacy with his bride.

Thai-Saing came upon them, introduced himself as an itinerant monk, and begged food and fellowship for the night in return for his prayers and his protection from the bandits that surely would follow the wagon tracks. The young groom realized his mistake in leaving the caravan. He might need the monk's protection. He granted Thai-Saing's wish, and bid Chen Shu-Chuan, his bride of sixteen, to prepare their food.

Thai-Saing could see that the girl was refined and educated. She sang to entertain them while they ate. Her voice and manners bore witness to her childhood care and teaching. The groom, on the other hand, seemed to have wealth, but he was not educated, and he was not in the same class as the girl. How was this union made possible? Thai-Saing inquired of the groom in confidence.

"I wish to bless your union. Tell me your circumstances that I may call upon Teng and Di."

"My family proposed our union to the Chen family. They sent assassins against us and killed my father and brothers. I alone escaped. I hired assassins to take Shu-Chuan by force and avenge my family. To avoid further bloodshed, she agreed to become my wife today, and we are fleeing the Chens. Please bless our first union tonight and our escape tomorrow."

"I will. In private, after we have finished eating."

They talked while Shu-Chuan tended the fire, ate, and put away the food. When the twilight was fading into darkness, Thai-Saing asked the boy to walk with him and pray. The groom complied, bowing to the wishes of the holy man.

At one hundred meters away from the campfire, Thai-Saing turned and hit the groom in the stomach with a force that dropped the boy to his knees, gasping for air. Thai-Saing forced him to the ground, tied his arms in back, and gagged him. He cut a length of cane, forced the boy's legs apart, and tied a foot to each end of the stalk.

He cut another stalk, sharpened it on both ends, stuck one end in the ground, and hoisted the groom's full weight upon the other. The groom's own weight and breathing began forcing the stick to cut its way into his chest as he watched Thai-Saing walk toward the fire and the waiting Shu-Chuan.

"Your husband has become overwhelmed with faith and repentance for his actions against your family. He has been inspired to begin a holy pilgrimage of contrition and has gone ahead of us on foot."

Shu-Chuan was upset and near tears. She was now alone and far from her family in this hostile province. Thai-Saing approached and comforted her.

"Have no fear. Your husband had consigned you into my care. I am bound by his covenant to guard you, to accompany you, and to care for you until we can rejoin him at the end of his pilgrimage. At that time, he will be a kind and honorable husband."

Shu-Chuan dried her tears and bowed low in resignation. Thai-Saing continued to counsel her. Question by question, he was gaining her confidence. He continued his probing inquiry.

"Have you been prepared for husbanding by a monk or your family?"

Being sheltered, shy, and knowing nothing of the ways of men, she confessed that she had not.

"No, holy one."

Thai-Saing had figured as much. She was naïve. She was completely innocent and unaware of the world about her. No such *preparation* existed to his knowledge.

"Your man has asked me to bless you, to care for you, and to bring you to him prepared to be a wife. I will prepare you to receive your husband."

She bowed and agreed to be prepared by the monk. With more wood added, the fire blazed with bright intensity, and the flickering light accentuated Shu-Chuan's frail beauty. Thai-Saing toyed with her, knelt beside her, undressed her, and consumed her innocence throughout the night, explaining how each touch, ever bolder and evermore satisfying, was but one lesson in preparing her to meet her husband at the end of his journey. These were the last images that were projected into the tear-filled eyes of the hapless groom.

Lin Thai-Saing took full possession of the girl, the wagon, and the groom's modest wealth. At dawn, sensing that the Chen family's assassins might be in pursuit, he ordered her to stay in the wagon and out of sight. Abandoning his original mission, he returned to Hong Kong and considered the pros and cons of how best to use his new acquisition.

Lin Wu would not be allowed to touch her. She would not be worked with the other girls. She was being prepared to join her husband, and her duties were to educate and teach the girls manners. From Shu-Chuan, they would learn to sing, to dance, to speak softly, and to please men.

On the outskirts of the city, he noticed that Lin Wu was waiting for him. Wu greeted his master.

"The dock officer came to me and asked for gold to keep silent about the two sailors."

"What did you do?"

"I lured him into the old warehouse where we met. Then, I killed him."

"Good. Then, why do you meet me here? And who is watching the girls?"

"The officer had reported you to his superiors. You are to be arrested and executed without a trial."

Thai-Saing had little choice. He boarded a ship, the only ship that was sailing that night. It carried cargoes of silks and spices and had accommodations for passengers. He paid the captain in gold for six passages and three cabins.

The ship was bound for the Bay of San Francisco in the Americas, then around Cape Horn to its homeport of Boston. Thai-Saing soon recovered his expenses when the other passengers and sailors found him to be an honorable man with respect to his wife, and strict with his younger brother, yet ...

> *"... a man who leans considerably leeward in accepting modest sums in exchange for the virtue of his three handsome sisters. Such magnanimity befriends the man to us all, and secures for us a very tranquil voyage."*
>
> *Logbook of the Polar Star*
> *November 15, 1848*

> *"Feb'y 15, 1851 ... Rec'd $50 in gold coin from Niccolo Vestoni of Dusino, Italy, three passages for himself, wife Sophia, and daughter Caralina, Panama to S.F."*
>
> *Logbook of the Polar Star*

> *"March 1, 1851 ... Sophia, beloved wife of Niccolo Vestoni, died of cholera last night. The men were saddened, as she had been trained in the opera and had sung for them on occasion. This morning we buried her at sea. The only sounds were the wind whipping the sails and the sobbing of the daughter, who remains inconsolable."*
>
> *Logbook of the Polar Star*

"... don't come to my bed looking for anything."

"What were you thinking? Why didn't you tell me?"

"I didn't think it was important."

"Not important? Running slaves in the *Polar Star* not important? How stupid. How mortifying. Our friends will shun us now."

"For a while, perhaps, but they'll come around."

"When did all of this take place?"

"In the thirties. Long before I knew you."

"For ten years? You ran slaves for ten years?"

"About that, yes."

"How did you get involved in that disgusting trade?"

"My father was captain of the *Polar Star*. He taught me."

"You told me he died in thirty-two."

"He did. The abolitionists shot him. I inherited his interest."

"And you continued to run slaves in it?"

"That's all I knew. The money was good, and I was able to buy out the other partners and buy stakes in other ships."

"Why did you stop?"

"We were flouting the laws. We could have been hanged. Commercial cargoes were becoming profitable, anyway. So, I converted my ships. I didn't have the stomach for slaving anymore."

"You didn't have the stomach? It took you ten years to figure that out?"

"No, it was ten years before I was in a position to do anything about it."

"You have four ships now. Sell it, Reef. Sell the *Polar Star*."

"No."

"It has a curse on it. Sell it. Let's move to Beacon Hill."

"No."

"This obsession of yours to own ships. What are you building, a navy?"

No. The more ships you own, the more security you have. In case you lose one."

"I've always lived on Beacon Hill. I want to go back. But we can't unless you sell one or two of these damned ships."

"No. That's out of the question."

"Then run the triangle again."

Reef was shocked to hear such a suggestion come from Robin's lips.

"What?"

"Put the *Polar Star* back to work in the triangle. If the money is as good as you say, then we'll be on Beacon Hill in no time. Do it, Reef? For me?"

"No. Slaving is against the law and it's too risky. Besides, I told you. I have no stomach for it."

"Then don't come to my bed looking for anything."

"I'll come to your bed anytime I please."

She knew that he would. He had before. Damn him. He was even better when he was angry with her. She would be flogged before she would ever tell him, though. She left the room and slammed the door.

He did not tell her the whole truth. He could not sell the *Polar Star.* In 1849, two of his four ships sailed around Cape Horn with full cargoes and failed to reach their destinations. Various ships sailing toward Boston at the same time reported sighting his ships along the West Coast of South America. After Panama, his ships dropped out of sight.

By 1850, no sightings of his two ships had been reported and they were presumed lost. In 1851, his brig, *Sea Wind,* failed to report. Again, no sightings north of Panama. When his fourth and last ship, *Polar Star,* failed to return from a voyage to Hong Kong, Reef sank into a pit of depression.

His junior partners in additional ships besieged him with their fears and anguish, and his creditors plagued him with financial demands. Reef sold his partnerships to cover some of his debts, but that was not enough. In a few months, everything that he had built was gone.

He was penniless. He had been stripped of his assets and his revenue. He awaited the legal action of his creditors, which was swift in coming.

"January 16, 1852 ... there being no sightings during the Period of Allowance prescribed by law, Polar Star is presumed lost at sea."

Record of Sightings
Boston Exchange Bank

"December 3, 1852 ... In re: Action of Insolvency, Boston Exchange Bank vs. Atherton, ... the court finds in favor of the plaintiff."

Superior Court
Commonwealth of Massachusetts

"Mr. Vestoni, you must sleep, now."

Lin Thai-Saing and Lin Wu walked in haste up Market Street, turned onto Geary, then down an alleyway, and entered the tenement where Niccolo Vestoni lived. A deep hacking cough could be heard as they approached. Thai-Saing knocked on the door.

"Come in," rasped Niccolo.

"Good day to you, Mr. Vestoni," responded the Chinaman as they entered. "I have brought your medicine, and the bond for you to sign."

Niccolo was dying of black lung disease, and Thai-Saing was concerned. He and Niccolo had talked many times about the dangers to be faced by his only daughter, Caralina, once the disease had claimed Niccolo. Thai-Saing was persistent and had demonstrated more than once that he had the money, position, and power to take care of her.

Niccolo had little choice but to accept the promises that Thai-Saing would be her guardian, would care for her, and would continue her musical education. For services that Caralina would render to Thai-Saing as his bonded domestic servant, Thai-Saing had agreed to pay Niccolo four hundred dollars in gold, with which Niccolo could pay for food, rent, and medicine.

Caralina was only ten, but she was well known in the slums of San Francisco. She was a radiant image of her mother, with raven black hair, deep dark brown eyes, a dainty nose, and dimples. She was personable, yet quiet, and had inherited her mother's angelic voice.

To her debit, she was attractive, far beyond the expectations of an adolescent, so much so that she would be a constant temptation to men. A fitting addition to the house of Lin Thai-Saing, and a worthy princess for his brothel.

Niccolo knew that Thai-Saing was a panderer of Chinese, Mexican, and Indian girls, but the Chinaman had befriended him for almost two years while scratching out a living in the slums. Thai-Saing had spotted them when they had first disembarked. He spoke their language. He had found them this hovel in which to live. He had found work for Niccolo as a stoker on the Oakland Ferry. He had brought them food many times, and clothing, and wood to burn in the winter. He had been a true friend, their only friend.

No civic group and no church had lifted a hand to help them. No one would look after Caralina now. The orphanages were filled with white Americans. Mexicans, foreigners, and Indians were not welcome. The churches made apologies and prayed for them, but gave no corporal assistance. Only Thai-Saing had pursued a consistent pattern of befriending Niccolo, with offers to educate and mentor the beautiful and talented child.

Niccolo knew that Thai-Saing was a married man who had great respect and reverence for his barren wife, Shu-Chuan. Perhaps the Chinaman saw in Caralina the daughter that Shu-Chuan could not give him. Niccolo was dying. He had little choice but to welcome the Chinaman into his home and into his confidence.

"Thank you, Mr. Lin. Sit down."

They sat. Caralina was kneeling, praying at her bedside, and weeping. Thai-Saing continued.

"Good day, Mr. Vestoni. I have brought the gold. Are you ready to issue Caralina's bond to me?"

Caralina continued to pray. Above the bed, a daguerreotype of her mother drew her attention, and her tears. Niccolo admonished her.

"Caralina. Dry your eyes. Mr. Lin is here to talk business."

"Yes, Papa. I'm sorry. I'm sorry. I miss Mama so."

"I know. I know. I miss her, too. But, I am sick, Caralina, and you know that I must talk to Mr. Lin now. He is going to take care of you when I am gone, and you must trust him and obey him."

"I won't cry anymore. Please forgive me, Papa. I will obey Mr. Lin, if you wish."

"Where do you go today, Caralina?"

"I'll go to the docks, Papa. I sell more bread there than anywhere, and sometimes more flowers, too. The passengers seem to have more money and better appetites."

"You must sing songs, too, Caralina. Your voice is beautiful. People love to hear you sing, and they will give you money. Money to buy my medicine."

"Yes, Papa. I will sing for them today."

"Sing for me, Caralina. One more time. Sing *Vaga Luna* for me."

She obeyed. The lyrics of the aria poured from her lips almost without effort, in a manner so lovingly taught to her by her mother. In a few moments, Caralina finished the aria and kissed her father.

"Go, then, child, and earn lots of money today. Money to buy food and shelter for us."

"Yes, Papa."

Caralina gathered her basket of bread and flowers, kissed her father again, curtsied to Thai-Saing and Wu, and left the room. Seeing that Niccolo's condition had turned for the worse since his visit the previous day, Thai-Saing wasted no time.

"I have brought the bond for you, Mr. Vestoni, and the gold. Four hundred dollars."

Niccolo reached for the sack of gold, but Thai-Saing withdrew it from his reach.

"But first, Mr. Vestoni, you must sign the bond."

Wu produced a pen and a bottle of ink. Thai-Saing opened the bottle, dipped the pen, and handed it to Niccolo. Without even reading the terms of the bond, Niccolo signed it and began counting the coins. He was immersed in his arithmetic when a knock sounded at the door. Wu opened it and Anita Travis entered the room.

"Oh, Mr. Vestoni. I didn't know anyone was here. Mimi made this custard for you. For your throat."

Niccolo greeted her.

"Come in Anita. You know Mr. Lin."

Anita was not pleased to see Lin Thai-Saing.

"Yes, sir. Good day, Mr. Lin."

Thai-Saing smiled and bowed to her. Anita continued.

"Mr. Vestoni?"

"Yes, Anita?"

"Caralina was crying outside. Why?"

"You should not worry about Caralina anymore. Mr. Lin is going to take care of her from now on."

Niccolo resumed his counting. Thai-Saing stepped forward, placing one hand on her shoulder. Stroking her hair with the other, he softened his voice.

"She will learn to be happy with me. She will sing. She will dance. You should let Lin Thai-Saing teach you, too."

He attempted to embrace her. She pulled away in anger as he continued. Thai-Saing continued to whisper.

"You're pretty like Caralina. You can sing and dance and buy pretty dresses, too."

Anita pulled farther away from the two Chinese. She looked at Niccolo. He was still counting the coins and seemed not to notice. She raised her voice to gain Niccolo's attention.

"Never. I'll starve first. I won't sing for you, and I won't be a whore for you. I'll die first."

Thai-Saing took her by the arm, turned his back on Niccolo, and placed his finger to his lips. He did not want the girl to interrupt Niccolo. He leaned forward, put his mouth to her ear, and spoke in a clear low tone.

"Think of your family. Look at their clothes. They have little food. You live in squalor. Show them that you love them. Come and sing your song for Lin Thai-Saing."

Anita was angry. She pushed herself free, jostling Thai-Saing. Wu moved to intercede. He grabbed Anita and held her off the floor against his torso. He looked to Thai-Saing for direction.

Thai-Saing shook his head, and gestured for Wu to release her. This was not the time or the place to take possession of this one. Her time would come later. His target was Caralina, and he was not to be distracted.

Wu looked at Anita, smiled, and held her closer, beyond the sight of Niccolo. He fondled her breasts and her pelvis as she struggled to break free. Then, he released her. She ran from the room and slammed the door behind her.

Niccolo's counting was interrupted by a bout of coughing. He was spitting up blood, trying to catch his breath, wheezing, and choking. Thai-Saing took the moment of opportunity to offer his help, his final offer to Niccolo. He bolted the door, caught Wu's gaze, and spoke to him in their native tongue.

"Help me move him to the bed. Then finish him."

Wu nodded. Thai Saing addressed the Italian.

"Mr. Vestoni, you must sleep now. Here. Lin Wu and I will assist you."

Together, they helped Niccolo to the bed. Thai-Saing held Niccolo's arms down on the pillow above his head. Lin Wu knelt with his full weight on

Niccolo's chest, and clamped his hands tightly over the sick man's nose and mouth.

Niccolo tried to struggle, but his strength was gone in a few moments. All was silent, and he was stilled forever. Thai-Saing waited a few moments to make sure that he was dead.

"Go. Get Caralina. Tell her that her father is dying. Tell her to come quickly. Go."

"Yes, Master."

Thai-Saing retrieved the gold and the bond from the table, pocketed them, then knelt in solemn prayer beside the bed of the dead Italian to await Caralina's sobbing entrance.

She burst into the room, saw her father's lifeless face, and screamed. She kneeled at his bed and sobbed. Thai-Saing put his hands on her shoulders to comfort her. In a few minutes, she found the strength to contain her grief.

Thai-Saing had witnessed little beauty in his violent life, but he was awed at the aria that Caralina began to sing to her father for the last time. *Vaga Luna* had been her father's favorite. She had learned it from her mother, who had learned it as a protégé of a maestro in Milano.

The clarity and tone of the child's voice belied her grief, and she filled the room with her rendition.

Thai-Saing was well pleased with his new acquisition.

"January 31, 1853 ... Coroner's Inquest
Name: Niccolo Vestoni
Residence: Dusino, Italy.
Date of Birth: Unknown
Date of Death: January 29, 1853
Cause of death: Consumption.
Disposition of Remains:
        Buried in Pauper's Cemetery"
                        Coroner's Record
                        City of San Francisco

"You will sing for me tonight ..."

Sunrises were the slowest times at Thai-Saing's love nest. After drinking, dancing, and whoring all night, none of the customers that had paid for the night of merriment was intent upon getting an early start on the new day. The girls who had worked the hardest were just as intent upon extending their stays with their unwashed partners, as long as they were allowed to sleep unmolested.

A few sailors and miners were still sleeping at the bar. The girls who had not earned their keep the night before were cleaning their empty cribs, the tables, and washing linens, glassware, and floors. Shu-Chuan demanded that the girls keep themselves and their home clean and neat, a discipline which few of them were inclined to practice on their own.

Caralina had been in Thai-Saing's stable for two months. He was not pleased with her revenue. He sat down at a table next to the dance floor. Shu-Chuan stood behind him. He scolded two young

Mexican girls and Caralina, and he left no doubt that
he was annoyed with Caralina.

"Your songs are lifeless, and your dances have
no beauty. Too many men pass you by. Without
paying. You have not learned the gentle ways of love.
You have not paid attention to Shu-Chuan."

"But my love," one of the Mexicans pleaded.
"There are too many girls. Older girls. They grab the
men before we can get them."

The other Mexican echoed the first.

"Girls with prettier dresses. Older girls are
mean. They push us against something to soil us and
then they laugh at us."

Thai-Saing was not convinced.

"And you, Caralina? What is your excuse"

"I try to please them, my love. I sing. I dance. I
try."

Thai-Saing slapped her in the face.

"I dress all of you. I feed all of you. You will
sing louder than the others. Sweeter. You will dance
closer. Touch more. Lift your skirts higher. Kiss the
men with wetter mouths. Bring more men into this
house of love."

"Yes, my love," they whimpered in separate
replies.

Thai-Saing turned to Caralina.

"I promised your father that I would take care
of you. Give you a home. Buy you clothes. If not for
Lin Thai-Saing, you would starve. You are so
ungrateful. What would your father say to you if he
were here?"

At the mention of her father, Caralina began to
cry. Thai-Saing knew how to use the memory of

Niccolo against her, and he used it often to suit his purposes. He turned to Shu-Chuan.

"You go now, my love. Teach them your songs. Teach them your dances and your gentle ways. Pay special attention to Caralina. Then, she will attract more men to her crib. And her crib will buy you a pretty new dress."

"You will sing for me tonight?" he asked Caralina.

"Yes, my love."

Lin Thai-Saing gave her a gentle slap, then turned her and pushed her onto the dance floor.

"Yes, my love." he mimicked. "You will. Now go and learn your dances, learn your songs, and learn the joy of making men spend their money for your love."

The two Mexicans forced smiles, bowed, and retreated. Caralina went to the middle of the dance floor, where Shu-Chuan and the girls began attending to her. They adjusted her dress, fixed her hair, and began their steps, accompanied by their tiny voices, singing a song in Spanish that Caralina had yet to learn. Caralina dried her tears, watched a minute, and then followed their steps with ease.

She loved to display herself in such a manner, like performing on a stage with people loving her innocent performances, yet unable to understand the connection between her actions and the motivations of the customers that she was being taught to entice.

She was much more beautiful and graceful than the two, or any of the other girls at the house for that matter, and much more studious. She enjoyed singing much more than the dancing, but she resigned herself to the task at hand, raised her arms, and began moving in step to the dance.

She moved her arms high above her head, as if to caress a tall man, moving them down his imaginary form, to caress his face, his shoulders, chest, waist, and his hips. What could she do to attract this man? What could she do to get his attention? He seems so cold. So unfeeling. Does he not feel the tears that drown her soul?

I am Caralina. A little girl. Won't you spend some time with me? I am not as pretty as the older girls you see. Their bodies bloom forth the grown-up things you seek. I know that you are busy. I know you have to go. No time for me. But, I am someone, too. I have feelings, too. I can tell them to you if you will let me. If only you will stop. Please stop. Come over here, and spend some time with me. Please, Mister. Please.

Would anyone ever love me again? Would anyone ever want to be my friend? The little girls that stand down from the beautiful ships. They are so soft and tender. So clean, so neat, and sweet. So well watched over by their mothers. Not allowed to speak to me. Or play with me. Even if I had a fine and precious doll to share. Which I do not.

Thai-Saing demanded that his girls train and practice their art. Harlots congregated along the wharves, offering intense competition that he demanded be met and beat. He insisted that each of his girls offer not only a dance or a song to a man, but also her smile, a provocative view up her dress, the contours of whatever breasts she boasted, the scent of her perfume, the taste of her kiss, and the warmth of her presence. These were the gifts given freely by the girls of Lin Thai-Saing, and they were the finest along the streets of San Francisco.

Let the other sluts on the street recite their "Two-bittee lookie, four-bittee feelie, six-bittee fuckie." Lin Thai-Saing's girls were in a class one order of magnitude above those slovens and he would have it no other way. Thai-Saing watched Shu-Chuan teach Caralina from his chair. How gentle they were with each other. How tender. How graceful their movements. He was pleased with what he saw. He would have them both tonight.

"April 12, 1853 ... Received of Lin Thai-Saing, $30.00, silk dress, custom order for Shu-Chuan."

> *Receipt from Mme. Louise*
> *Seamstress*

"*Well*, *I'm here, aren't I?*"

The San Francisco docks at nighttime were a frenzy of activity whenever a ship docked, Even in the rain, even in the bitter cold wind. If there was no room at the dock, then the crew made fast to the outboard side of the ship that was already docked.

All of the traffic was one way, from the ship to the gold fields. The cold be damned. The rain be damned. Anything that got in the way was trampled asunder.

Passengers and crew alike were getting off in a rush, glad to be free of their boredom and their tight quarters. Sometimes, even the captain and officers rushed to the gangplanks, abandoning the cargo in the holds. In spite of the persistent drizzle and cold wind, whiskey drummers, pick-and-pan peddlers, room-for-the-night hawkers, prostitutes, and thieves alike swarmed to the docks, eager to relieve the passengers of their money. Those passengers who appeared well dressed were prized targets of opportunity.

Dr. Ellis Trowbridge was well dressed. So were his two wives, Madelaine and Beth Ellen. They served as his nurses and they were superior in the practice of their vocation. They loved to assist Ellis in surgery of any kind, on man or beast, despite the screaming and howling. While Beth Ellen loved sewing and reading, Madelaine loved singing and music. Their talents were a perfect blend for the likeable portly doctor.

Trowbridge left his wives and their bundles on the dock by the gangplank. He instructed them to engage a porter with a cart, while he proceeded toward the street to hire a carriage. Caralina spotted his fine clothes and approached him. She reached up, put her arms around him, kissed him with moist rouged lips, and began to sing and dance.

"A handsome man. A gentle man.
A lonely man in need.
You need a lover for the night.
Let Caralina lead.
I'll sing for you. Dance for you.
Tell me what you want
And I'll be yours."

Trowbridge was speechless. He gazed at her with an embarrassing measure of desire. Prostitutes had approached him before, but not within sight and earshot of his wives; nor had one ever been such a beautiful child. Caralina held his hands in hers and continued to sing to him as she pulled him toward Thai Saing's brothel.

Madelaine saw them, kept her distance, and listened to the girl sing. Beth Ellen approached with a porter, and she lost no time in announcing her presence by taking Trowbridge's arm and forcing Caralina to release his hands.

Madelaine was moved by her song, and pained by the girl's mist-soaked hair and clothing. Seeing Beth Ellen, Caralina began a swift retreat, and bumped into Madelaine. Caralina turned and faced Madelaine, who held her fast. Caralina was frightened and began searching for Thai-Saing or Wu. Madelaine addressed her with tenderness in her voice.

"Don't go. That was a lovely song you were singing. Will you sing it for me again?" asked Madelaine.

Caralina was scared. "I'm sorry. I didn't mean anything. I'll sing for you if you'll let me go."

"You're so young. What are you doing here?"

Caralina began to cry. "I'm sorry, ma'am. I don't mean anything by it. I'm sorry. Please let me go. I'll get into trouble."

"My dear, you're wet and cold. Can't you get out of this weather and put on some dry clothes?" Madelaine persisted.

"No, ma'am. Please let me go, now."

"Why are you here? What do your kinfolk think about you being down here?"

Caralina squirmed, jerked, and broke free, responding with her tears.

"Well, I'm here, aren't I?"

She made good her escape and was soon lost in the crowd. Lin Wu had been watching her. Seeing no immediate threat from the three passengers, he allowed the little scene to play itself out. Madelaine was not satisfied with the outcome, however, and was saddened by the girl's departure.

"Ellis, who is this Caralina? Who is she?"

Trowbridge sensed that an inquisition was imminent, that he would be the accused, and was therefore brief with his answer.

"I don't know, my dear. Honest, I do not know."

"Oh, Ellis. She's so pitiful. Can't we help her?"

Trowbridge was pleased to hear that she was concerned only with the girl and not his culpability. He was relieved that he was acquitted, and he responded with focused tenderness.

"Yes, my dear, I suppose we can. Do you want me to try and find her?"

"Oh, yes, Ellis. Please do. Find her and let us help her."

"Yes, my dear. I'll go and find her."

Indeed, he wanted to find her again. She had stirred feelings within him that would be embarrassing and difficult to explain to his elders and his bishop. Yes, he wanted to find her, but he could not.

Madelaine waited for her husband to return, peering down the girl's presumed path. Strains of Caralina's song still filled her ears. She repeated to herself the words from the girl's lips that had touched her.

"Well, I'm here, aren't I?"

Trowbridge returned a few minutes later, shrugged his shoulders at his wives, and proceeded to hire a carriage. The porter and driver loaded the luggage as they climbed aboard. Trowbridge paid the porter, then stared at other sing-song girls who were pawing their potential customers.

The driver released the brakes, loosened the reins, and drove them away. Only Madelaine turned to take one last look, as if to make one final search for the urchin that had, for only a brief and fleeting moment, so completely filled her childless heart with joy.

> *"March 12, 1853 ... Boarded a ship in New Orleans for Panama on the tenth of this instant. Today, we were accosted by monogamists, who threatened to jettison us. A Mr. Charles Boles claimed no religious affiliation, and yet he intervened in our behalf."*
> *Ellis Trowbridge*
> *Letter to Bishop Jennings Hartley*

> *"June 4, 1853... Arrived safely San Francisco yesterday despite extreme discomforts and frequent insults. Four men died on the way. I could not help them for they refused to boil their water.*
> *The Saints continue to drink boiled water, and the Catholics drink beer and wine. Both congregations seem equally healthy, Scriptures notwithstanding.*
> *Prostitutes and all manner of questionable merchants accosted us upon standing down from the ship. My heart urges any Saint who runs this gauntlet to keep his companions and his wives close to him for spiritual guidance and succor."*
> *Ellis Trowbridge*
> *Letter to Bishop Jennings Hartley*

" *You might have waited until he left town ...*"

Passengers were lined up and waiting to board the train to New York as it backed into the Boston station. It was late, as usual, and the conductor was in a hurry, as usual. He signaled for all passengers to board. Reef hugged Robin for a long time. Then, he kissed her goodbye. Robin tears flowed without shame. She took a little package from her purse, and handed it to Reef.

"What's this?"

"Just so you won't forget me."

"Don't be silly. I'll find my ships and rebuild an entire fleet for you. I'll be back within a year, and I'll buy you the most fashionable house on Beacon Hill."

Reef took the package and stored it inside his coat pocket. He kissed her again, then he picked up his bulging sea bag, and walked toward the train. Robin walked back toward the station. She turned, looked back at the train, caught Reef's eye, and waved to him as he boarded.

Deep within, Robin was furious. Reef had escaped. She had not even suspected that he was planning a trip, much less an odyssey to search for his stupid ships. What had possessed him? She had to find a way to bring him back to her. If she could have her way, he was going to be a banker. Like her father. She would find a way to bring him back.

In the shadows of the station, concealed from view of the train, Paul Duchard stood at ease and leaned against a pillar with his arms folded. When Robin turned to wave goodbye to Reef, she found herself facing Paul. She was not surprised, and she was not annoyed, for she knew his intentions. Duchard was overjoyed to see Reef depart. Although she understood Paul's motivation, she felt that his presence was a little premature.

"You might have waited until he left town."

Duchard remained out of view of the train, leaned against the building, and faced Robin, smiling in anticipation of the future.

The passenger car was dirty, noisy, and crowded with passengers stowing their bundles and settling in for the long trip. Reef made his way along the aisle and spotted the last remaining seat at the end of the car. Seated across the aisle was a young messenger, with a large carpetbag resting beside him on the window seat.

A small white-on-blue "Express" sign hung from a nail above him. One arm rested on his lap and the other rested inside his coat. He was wide-awake, observing the entraining procession. Reef knew better than to ask him to move the bag and give up the window seat. Instead, he pointed to the empty seat.

"Is this seat taken?"

"No, I don't think so," replied the messenger.

The messenger's manner and tone were pleasant, but his gaze and attention was not distracted for an instant. The train jolted and began to move. Reef put his sea bag in the rack above and took the seat. The car was cold, so he did not remove his coat. He settled in as much as the tight quarters would allow, and prepared to get some sleep. Feeling the bulge in his coat pocket, he reached for Robin's gift and opened it.

It was a daguerreotype photograph of her, in a maroon *Union* case. To Reef, she was the epitome of perfection. Indeed, if there was a God, and He was tempted to give up His kingdom, He would give it up for Robin's love. For no other woman and for no other reason. Reef's yearning for her always surfaced whenever he saw her. Looking at her photograph was no exception. He sensed that this photograph would be his sole constant companion in the months to come.

He touched the image of her hair, her forehead, her nose, and her lips. He touched the soft maroon velvet and the gold filigree mat, and advanced his forefinger onward to the *V* in her dress, and the gold chain and locket she always wore with it. He looked at her for a full minute, closed the case, and put it away. He closed his eyes, and let the chuffing of the locomotive talk to him, and put words in her mouth for him, words that only he could hear, and words that she must be saying to him at this very moment.

"Reef. My Reef. I love you, Reef. My darling, Reef. Come back to me. My husband. Soon. Come back. Soon. Come back. Soon. Come back."

The locomotive continued to talk to him without ending, repeating for him over and over the words that he longed to hear from her lips. Soon he was fast asleep, and the locomotive continued its discourse with its other passengers, no one in particular, each one in turn, and every one in his own private world, repeating the words that each of them wanted most to hear.

Except for the messenger, every passenger in the car was sleeping as the train slowed to a stop. Two men opposite the messenger and seated facing the rear of the train, stirred from their deep sleep, shook themselves awake, got up and left, making way for three oncoming passengers. Three seats were available if the carpetbag were removed and stowed.

The first passenger moved past the messenger and reached for the carpetbag. The messenger put a restraining hand up, and his right hand moved deeper into his coat to grip the pistol at his waist. He was polite and firm, but gave the distinct impression that there would be no negotiation.

"I'm sorry, but this seat is taken."

"What do you mean, 'taken?' Do you expect us to sit on the floor?"

"I'm sorry, sir, but the ticket on this seat is paid through to New York. Perhaps you can find a seat in another car."

At this point, the second passenger stood squarely before the messenger as the train started with a jolt.

"How would you like us to throw you and your ticket-paying carpetbag off the train?"

By this time, Reef had awakened and appraised the situation. He spoke in a pleasant tone, and sounded a little sleepy, but there was no mistaking his meaning.

"Mister, find another seat, so we can get some sleep. You're making a big mistake trying to take that seat."

"Why is that?"

"Read the sign. He's a messenger, and the bag contains valuables. His hand isn't reaching for a handkerchief, I'll warrant you. If you try and take that bag from the seat, he'll kill you."

"There are three of us," offered the second man. The third man moved forward, as if to punctuate the second's statement.

Reef put his hand inside his coat and pretended to go back to sleep. His tone was firm and his meaning was clear.

"Find another seat. I'm not reaching for a handkerchief either."

The three passengers froze, stared at Reef, then at the messenger. After a long silence, the first passenger elbowed the second, who elbowed the third, and all three left the two vacant seats behind. The messenger removed his hand from his coat. He watched the three men until they left the car, and then he turned to Reef.

"I appreciate that, mister. More than you know. You didn't have to do that."

Getting a smile and nod, but no remark, he motioned toward Reef's coat.

"Were you bluffing?"

Reef sat up, smiled, and revealed his rigid forefinger with his thumb at full-cock. He released the thumb, then returned the forefinger to its imaginary holster.

"No. You weren't bluffing either, were you?"

"No." The messenger extended his hand. "My name is Sam Carson. Thanks again."

Reef shook Carson's hand.

"Atherton. Reef Atherton."

"Can I repay the favor in some way?"

Reef thought a moment, then laughed. "Thank you, yes. You can wake me up when we get to New York."

Carson laughed in reply. "I will. And I'll keep an eye on your sea bag while you're asleep. What do you do in New York?"

"I'm taking a ship to California."

"Gold fever?"

Reef was pensive, and his voice saddened. "No. My ships failed to report. I have to find them and get rich. So I can buy a wife."

"Is she a bonded servant?"

Reef was silent a moment and responded.

"No. Just expensive."

Reef tipped his hat down over his eyes, settled in, and prepared to sleep. Carson wondered about the man. What would possess him to enter a fight that was not his? A fight that could mean severe injury or death. To help a total stranger. He studied Reef for a few minutes, then returned to his own thoughts.

"June 12, 1853 ... A Mr. Atherton sided with me against three men who attempted to move the grip bag. My offer to show appreciation was refused."
Carson
Run Report
Boston & New York Express

"I've jacked, rigged, and bosuned ships like this."

Captain Lawson and first mate Singleton were seated at a table on the quarterdeck of the brig, *Tradewinds*, attending to a line of unruly drummers, crew applicants, and prospective passengers. Pushing, shoving, and arguments erupted frequently, since passenger space was limited and the demand was high.

Ahead of Reef, a rum drummer poured a shot from a jug into a small tin cup and offered it to Lawson. Lawson was a staunch Presbyterian and waved off the cup, deferring to his first mate.

"Mr. Singleton, if you please."

Singleton was no staunch anything, and was pleased to taste the rum.

"Aye, Cap'n," he obeyed, swished it around, and gulped it down.

"Ahh. It'll make a fine grog, Cap'n."

Lawson was more interested in his ship's stores than in Singleton's appraisal of the rum's blending quality.

"How many barrels have we stowed for this passage?"

"None yet, Cap'n."

Lawson pointed to the ship's log for the mate to enter the transaction. Singleton nodded and Lawson turned to the drummer.

"How much for four barrels?"

"Seventeen dollars apiece."

"I'll give you fifteen. I'll have four barrels for the crew. Mr. Singleton, see to possession and stowage."

"Aye, Cap'n."

Lawson was in a mood to dispense with formalities and move on to the next in line.

"Deliver them to Mr. Singleton today. We sail with the morning tide."

"Thank ye, Cap'n. I'll get them now."

The rum drummer reached for the jug. Lawson restrained him.

"This'll do for the plum duff, if it's as good as Mr. Singleton seems to think. The men need a good feed on the first night out."

The peddler released his grip on the jug.

"Enjoy your pudding, Cap'n."

"I will, drummer. Mr. Spuds. I say, Mr. Spuds."

Spuds was loading provisions into the galley. He wiped his hands in his apron, and came to the table.

"Aye, Cap'n?"

"See that this gets in your pudding tomorrow night."

"My pleasure, Cap'n," replied Spuds as he took the jug. Lawson restrained him, too.

"All of it. Lest you be reeking of it at the dogwatch."

"No, Cap'n, ... that is, ... Aye, Cap'n."

As Spuds disappeared with the jug, the captain addressed Reef.

"Next."

"I'm seeking sea duty, Cap'n. My name is Atherton. I'm good with a marlinspike. I helped rig this ship when she was fitting out. I can worm, parcel, and serve, or lash and splice as the need arises."

"This ship was rigged in New Orleans. Are you old Amos Atherton's son?"

"Aye, Cap'n. Amos was my father. I've just arrived from Boston, and I'm seeking passage to California."

Reef knew better than to mention his former command and ownership of the *Polar Star*. If Lawson had known Amos, then he would know of the *Polar Star*'s cargoes and his father's fate. If Lawson had liked Amos, Reef would be hired. If Lawson's sympathies were with the abolitionists, Reef would have to look elsewhere. That was understood.

Lawson looked Reef up and down, as if measuring him for a suit of clothes.

"Mr. Singleton."

"Aye, Cap'n?"

"This is Mr. Atherton. He says he's a rigger. Are we still in need of a bosun?"

"Aye, Cap'n. He'll earn his ration on this passage."

Lawson turned to Reef.

"Mr. Atherton, you'll take orders from Mr. Singleton. This ship is stoutly rigged. See that it stays that way."

"Thank you Cap'n. I will."

"One dollar and one ration a day. Share a bunk when you can find one. One ration of grog at the end of your watch. Put your mark in the book. Next."

Reef signed the roster, picked up his sea bag and went below deck with Singleton.

In the early morning, Captain Lawson and Singleton assembled the crew on deck for departure. A few passengers were up early, watching the activity. After Lawson signed for the cargo, the shipping company's officer disembarked. Lawson wasted no time in barking orders.

"Mr. Singleton, secure the gangway and prepare to cast off."

"Aye, Cap'n. Secure the gangway! Prepare to cast off!"

Some of the crewmen were already climbing the ratlines toward the yardarms, to be in position to untie and unfurl the sails. Others on deck were straining at the topping-lifts, preparing to raise the yards on the masts. Dockhands were removing the gangway.

"Cap'n, gangway secured. Ready to cast off."

"Mr. Singleton, cast off the bow lines."

"Aye, Cap'n. Cast off the bow lines!"

Crewmen released the lines, and pushed the bow away from the dock with gaffs.

"Mr. Singleton, cast off all lines and back the jib."

"Aye, Cap'n. Cast off amidships! Cast off stern! Starboard your helm!"

The steerman turned the wheel. They were under way.

"Mr. Singleton, Make all sail and lively now."

"Aye Cap'n. Starboard watch, set your main and make off. Port watch, man the starboard braces and stand by to haul away. Now, heave hearty, lads, and sing out. Sing out.

The second mate began the chantey. The crewmen responded in chorus, and pulled on the heavy lines in unison at each *pull*, *heave*, and *haul* in the chant.

> "Oh pull me from my bonnie bride.
> Pull me from my lovely sweetheart.
> Pull me from the girls I love.
> Pull, and go to sea again.
>
> Haul my lads, my bride is here.
> Haul my lassie's there beside her.
> Haul and give *ONE* hearty wave.
> Haul, and go to sea again.
>
> Heave. I love my bonnie bride.
> Heave. I also love my sweetheart.
> Heave and may they NEVER meet.
> Heave, and go to sea again.

The crewmen aloft unfurled the sails as the yards reached their position on the masts, and the wind filled each sail as soon as it was unfurled. Crewmen and passengers alike turned for a last look at New York harbor. For some of these men, Robin's morbid prophecy would indeed manifest itself. They would never return.

Tens of thousands of men had preceded the men on this same voyage. And tens of thousands would follow them. Hundreds would simply vanish, and their families would never know what had become of them.

Reef's days were spent high in the rigging with the ship in full sail hitting the white-capped swells that sprayed upon the decks below. He felt at home here, the only home that he had ever really known. The higher, the better, far above the monotony of the decks below. The task of splicing, or tarring parcels, and serving the weakened cordage of a frayed shroud or ratline was never-ending.

Twice during the voyage, he joined his crewmen on the decks for a service. With heads bowed, crewmen raised a plank, and the remains of a man would slide off and into the water. Passengers and crewmen were treated alike, as remains could not be preserved, and wood could not be spared for coffins.

Invariably, the man's pockets had been emptied, robbed by the one who had discovered the corpse. Only an entry in the captain's log noted the man's description and marked his passing from this earth for any one that cared to inquire. More often than not, no one cared.

At night, Reef had no trouble getting to sleep. As if performing a sacred ritual, he took the *Union* case from the pocket over his heart, opened it, and let his fingertip caress the image of Robin's hair, then her forehead, her nose, and her lips. He was saddened. He touched her image to his lips, closed the case, put it back in his breast pocket, then rolled over, and went to sleep.

From his quest, he never wavered. Despite his longing for Robin and home, he would not give up. He would find his ships. He would not go back to her a pauper. He would die first.

Reef was awakened by a loud and clear "Land ho!" one morning, followed by a rousing cheer from the crew and passengers. A long eight weeks away from New York and the sight of Colón meant that the journey was half over.

The crew was already furling the sails when Reef reached the deck. The deck hands began lowering the longboats that would tow the ship into the harbor. Passengers filled the decks to view the sight of land, making it almost impossible for the crew to secure the ship for docking.

Passengers disembarked first, leaving the crew aboard to await their pay and the captain's final inspection. Upon receipt of payment, each man grabbed his gear and sprang for the gangplank, eager to begin the twenty-mile trip to Panama City.

The dock was a flurry of activity, crowded with peddlers of food, drink, supplies and maps, men, children, and animals for hire with wagons, horses, mules, and donkeys, priests giving blessings to those with eternal and spiritual needs, and prostitutes attending to the temporal and not-so-spiritual needs.

Other than food and boiled water, buying supplies and maps in Panama was unnecessary. Only one path through the swamps and jungles led to Panama City, and it was filled with the men and their animals, carts, and wagons. Boats for hire could ply the rivers part of the way, making the journey much easier for those who had money. All were headed in the same direction, with the exception of a few returning home.

The majority of those returning was well dressed and rode animals, giving evidence of their new-found wealth. Most of the men going in the direction of Panama City were walking.

Reef did not need to check his billfold. He had the money to rent an animal or hire a boat, but he had decided to spend as little as possible. He began walking the slushy trail with everyone else. The line of sweating travelers was visible on into the hills, a never-ending string of humanity, not much different than a trail of ants.

The voracious mosquitoes competed with the ravenous flies for the blood of the gold seekers and provided the only sound to harmonize with the tramping of feet along the trail.

The sun and rain clouds were constant companions of the throngs of men on the trail. The sweltering heat competed with the torrential rains a half dozen times that day. Each time, no one took cover. Where a stretch of road bared its soil from underneath the jealous jungle, the parade of shoes and boots raised a cloud of dust. That day, the dust turned into mud a half dozen times. The men tramped through the mud each time until it literally turned back into dust.

Reef slogged through the mud along with the others, and climbed the last hill. He looked down upon the Pacific Ocean, and the harbor filled with passengers and crews boarding ships bound for San Francisco. Not one of the ships was his.

He made his way to the harbor and selected a brig with stout rigging. He approached the captain standing at the gangplank of the *Breakers*.

"Captain, my name is Atherton. Are you looking for sailors?"

"It depends, Mr. Atherton. What can you do?"

"Everything. I've jacked, rigged, and bosuned ships like this. I can reef, hand, and steer, and I can even cook if necessary."

"August 13, 1853 ... "Reef Atherton of Boston appt'd bosun, st'd rate, Panama to S.F."

Ship's Roster
Breakers

" ... Go on ahead, jack. I'll take care of the dishes. "

Reef's first glimpse of San Francisco was at dusk, when *Breakers* entered the bay, and the captain ordered the gun crew to fire the cannon.

Taking his cue, the ship's telegrapher hoisted his lantern to the crow's nest and began signaling the ship's manifest to the runners and merchandise brokers high on Telegraph Hill. When a single cargo item had been communicated to shore, Reef could see brokers dispatching runners down the hill and into the city.

Businessmen were desperate for news, inventory, and raw materials of any kind, and they were more than willing to pay the brokers and runners. The merchant who got to the dock first stood to strike the first and best bargain with the incoming ship's captain, to the exclusion and frustration of his competitors.

The wharves were crowded. The passengers were excited, loud, and rowdy. They were the first to leave, while the crew waited for its pay. Then, it was pandemonium with unity of thought: To leave the ship, buy some supplies, and find transportation to the gold fields.

Bars, brothels, and suppliers' shops abounded, many with entrances cut into the hulls of grounded and abandoned ships. Sing-song girls danced for the men. A few passengers stopped to take advantage of their services, then disappeared with them into the passageways and doors cut into the landlocked ships.

Anita stood beside her small wagon, trying to stay out of the way. She offered custards, bread loaves, and pies to passers-by that looked hungry. And everyone was hungry. Sailing ships abounded with salty stews and hard breads, and a fresh custard or pie for five cents was well within even the poorest man's budget.

A few feet away from Anita stood her friend, Caralina. Caralina approached Reef, who had fallen behind his crewmates and for the moment was standing alone. He was an attractive man. Cleaner than most. She approached him with the alluring movements and song that might be expected of a girl twice her age.

> "Follow me, now, my love.
> I am little Caralina, and I sing.
> Sing a sweet song of love.
> A little time with me will bring
> A little love to you tonight."

Reef was speechless. She began to sing and move to her song's rhythm, touching Reef here and there as she circled him, taking him by his free hand, and beckoning him to follow her.

"Let me sing my song for you.
And tell you of my yearning.
Sing this night away with me.
And we'll be one 'til morning."

He was very attractive. Maybe he had money and maybe he didn't, but he was attractive. She wet her forefinger and raked it slowly across Reef's lips. He felt the moisture, grabbed her hand, and smelled the perfume that she wore. He was shocked and angered. Not so much at her behavior, but at her tender age. He scolded her and shook her.

"No. You're just a child. What are you doing here? Where is your father?"

She reacted with fear at Reef's reproach. She saw Thai-Saing, Wu, and a miner approaching. Thai-Saing was intent upon putting her to work and paid no attention to Reef. Thai-Saing licked his thumb and forefinger, transferred five pinches of gold dust from the miner's gold poke to his own, and handed the former back to the miner. The miner stowed his poke and reached to take Caralina.

"You come and sing for me, pretty one."

Reef restrained the miner.

"Just a minute. You can't do that. I'm talking to her."

"You're wrong, jack. I can do that. Caralina's mine, tonight. You find someone else."

Reef pushed the miner away from Caralina. Wu intervened, took Reef from behind, spun him around, and hit him. Wu hit him again and again in the stomach, face, and head, forcing Reef to retreat. Reef had been taken by surprise and was no match for the bodyguard.

Wu continued to hit him, and with one final blow, knocked him backward, toppling Anita's wagon, and onto the ground. Loaves of bread and dishes of pie and custard went flying. The miner had enjoyed the show. He laughed, retrieved Caralina, kissed her on the mouth, and carried her down a passageway between the abandoned ships.

Reef came to, groggy, stunned, and blinded. He was struggling to breathe, and unable to pick himself up. His nose and mouth were bleeding, and his hair and face were matted with pie and custard.

"She's so young. She shouldn't be here. She's just a child."

Anita had watched Wu lead the miner and Caralina to a lighted door. After they entered, Wu closed it, turned, and stood watch outside. Anita was accustomed to life in the streets. For five pinches of gold dust, the miner had purchased one hour in private quarters with her little friend.

During those moments, he could and would satisfy any fantasy, lust, and the highest comfort to which his imagination could aspire. Wu would then reclaim Thai-Saing's princess, and offer her to the next passing miner or mariner.

Anita knew that she and the stranger were powerless to stop the cruelty. Caralina had reached the age of consent, and if her domestic bondage was questioned, Thai-Saing had learned long ago that a few dollars in a judge's pocket, or a gratuitous union with Caralina, would resolve any issue.

For Caralina, a question was begged. Who was this man? He had been kind to her. He had mentioned her beloved father, not to extract something from her as Thai-Saing did, but in kindness, like the pretty lady a few weeks ago. No man had ever tried to restrain another from using and hurting her, unless it was to settle an argument about who would be first. How she wished that this tall and handsome stranger had paid the five pinches of gold.

Reef was anguished by what he had witnessed. Still, he could not move. Wu knew his craft of protecting Caralina and punishing any man who would dare usurp his authority over her. Wu's eyes searched up and down the passageway for any signs of trouble, and frequently glanced over and fixed upon Reef.

Reef was still dazed and dizzy. Anita took a cloth and dabbed blood from Reef's mouth and chin, and wiped custard from his eyes, face, and hair. He took the cloth and protested aloud.

"Why is she here? Why does she do that?"

"She does that to eat. That's how she lives."

"But her parents. Why do they let her do that?"

"She belongs to Lin Thai-Saing, the Chinaman. She's an immigrant. Her father bonded her over to him before he died. The law protects him, and his bodyguard sees that no one interferes."

"Bodyguard?"

"Lin Wu. The one that hit you."

"Why did her father do that?"

"They're Italians. Poorhouses and churches don't care about immigrants. She and her father were alone and he was dying. If she were alone, she wouldn't last a week. Someone would cut her throat, steal her money, and dump her body in the bay."

Anita was blunt, but her assessment was correct. Social consciousness was a pastime of the Eastern wealthy leisure class. The inhabitants of San Francisco town were hell bent upon acquiring gold any way that they could get it, and they would find an immigrant child prostitute an easy target.

Reef was beginning to get a sense of balance. He sat up. Anita helped him to his feet and continued.

"Three or four bodies are found in the bay each week. Mostly men, but occasionally a sing-song girl, too. You could have wound up there, yourself, if this had been a dark, deserted passageway. What you did was very foolish. They will remember you, now."

Lin Thai-Saing was still observing Reef and Anita. Seeing that Wu was standing outside the bolted door, and that Reef had been subdued, he studied the sailor who had attempted the gallant gesture toward Caralina. He did not like public brawls between men over his girls. He detested any pious and sanctimonious stranger that took an interest in the welfare of his girls. He would remember this man's face. Giving Anita and Reef one final glance, he turned and walked out of the passageway to the street and into his house of comforts.

By this time, the last group of crewmen from the *Breakers* was leaving the ship. They were in good spirits, and they approached arm-in-arm, singing a chantey, and embracing and kissing any available sing-song girls. When they spotted Reef, they altered their sway and their path to absorb him and Anita into their celebration.

Anita was aware of their intentions and moved away. Their momentum enveloped Reef, and moved him from a standing position to a jaunty walk in step with them, away from Anita, and down the street toward the stage office. Anita stayed behind and watched him go. Seeing him disappear into the crowd, and seeing that he had no intention of paying for the mess that he had created, she yelled after him.

"Oh, sure. You go on ahead, jack. I'll take care of the dishes."

She looked at the pies on the street and the custard smeared over her best dress and began to cry.

"Happy birthday, Anita."

Indeed, Reef was oblivious to Anita's commercial disaster, but he was still troubled about Caralina, and he tried to enlist the help of his mates.

"There's a little girl in that ship. They're raping her."

One of his mates was sympathetic, but offered no assistance.

"These streets are full of urchins, Reef. You'll get used to it."

"But a man paid gold for her. She's only a child."

"It beats starving. That's the way it is here. You want to buy her? Then buy her. They're all for sale. One hundred dollars for the ugly ones, and the price goes up from there, but then, you'll have to feed her and take care of her. You got that kind of money?"

The mate was right. For as little as one hundred dollars in gold, any man could buy a sing-song girl from her owner. No record was made of the transaction, and the new owner could take her to the camps and prostitute her to recover his investment. He could force her to marry him, beat her unmercifully, and work her to death. If she died, he would bury her without ceremony in an unmarked grave, or throw her remains down a deep gorge to be eaten by animals. Another trip to San Francisco town would provide a convenient replacement. All for one hundred dollars.

Reef did not have that kind of money. His mate's admonitions reminded him that he was there to find his ships, and not to spend money redeeming the bondage contracts of indigent children. At his mates persistent tugging, Reef went along with them to the street, past the entrance to Thai-Saing's brothel, and toward the stage office.

He turned to take a parting look, as if to mark the spot for an eventual return. What he saw stunned him, halted his gait, and separated him for good from his former shipmates. He stood in silence, sickened by what he saw.

Thai-Saing's house of pleasure and dozens of other bars, whore houses, and mercantiles were in fact the hulls of ships that had been abandoned at the docks by their avaricious crews that were bound for the gold fields. These ships rested in the sands and dirt fills without their masts and without their rigging, stripped, looted, and condemned even while dirt was being hauled to fill in the passageways between them. They had been auctioned to the one, two, or three bidders present.

Each ship had been built and registered in a distant port and given a name. Reef was staring at the name. On this ship, the pleasure house of Lin Thai-Saing, the name carved in faded gold and green letters was *Polar Star*.

> *"September 20, 1853 ... the ship Polar Star is hereby declared a menace to navigation, not seaworthy, and a Public Annoyance. Therefore, being duly billed for auction as prescribed by law, the Polar Star is hereby sold to Lin Thai-Saing for the sum of one hundred dollars."*
>   *Record Of Condemnations*
>   *Harbormaster, San Francisco*

*"F*ind this Atherton. Follow him."

Shu-Chuan escorted the judge of the Superior Court to a soft chair in Thai-Saing's chambers in the stern of the *Polar Star.* A girl brought the judge his favorite whiskey and a glass. Thai-Saing entered and closed the door as the girl left.

"Good evening, your honor. How may I be of service?"

"Just thought you'd like to know. Someone has been asking about the *Polar Star.*"

"What about the *Polar Star?*"

The judge cast his eyes toward Shu-Chuan. Thai-Saing reassured him.

"She understands little English and does not concern herself with the ways of men. You may speak freely."

"A fellow by the name of Atherton. Apparently your man roughed him up yesterday."

"Yes, I remember him. What was he asking?"

"He wants to know the causes of action that we used to condemn his four ships and sell them. He claims that *Polar Star* was one of the four. He's planning to go to court to get it back."

"Your laws and courts are most unkind to our people, especially when your people file actions against us. We always lose. Would he bring his action into your court?"

"Yes, it would be in my court initially."

"What can you do?"

"I can require him to post an exorbitant bond to inhibit the action."

"Then, please do it. He has the look of a pauper. He could not possibly post a large bond. What can I offer you in return?"

"Caralina."

"Caralina?"

"For the night."

Thai-Saing stared at the judge. Both men smiled Thai-Saing turned to Chen Shu-Chuan.

"Get Caralina. And Wu."

She bowed and departed on her errand. Thai-Saing thanked the judge for his information. In a few moments, the three entered the chambers. Thai-Saing took the young girl's hand and walked her to the judge's chair.

"Take the judge to your crib tonight and sing for him. He is an honored guest and must be treated with love and respect."

"Yes, my love," replied Caralina.

She took the judge's hand and led him from the room. When the door closed, Thai-Saing proceeded to the desk and retrieved the logbooks of the *Polar Star*. These were the symbols of his ownership and he was the master of the *Polar Star.* How dare anyone challenge his authority? He raised and shook the logbooks at Wu and Shu-Chuan.

"First he casts his eyes upon Caralina. Now, he becomes obsessed with claiming my entire house."

He threw the logbooks down on the desk and continued to rant. He looked at Wu.

"Get two good men. Find this Atherton. Follow him. Find out where he goes. Then, have the men bring word back to me."

> *"Sept 27, 1853 ... In re Atherton v. Lin, bond is set at fifteen hundred dollars, payable prior to further adjudication ... "*
> *Clerk of the Superior Court*
> *City of San Francisco*

" ... Nuggets ... lying there. Waiting to be taken."

Gold. Seven nuggets in all. Heavy. Resting in his palm. Each one was the size of a kernel of corn. Reef agitated and manipulated each one again and again with thumb and forefinger, as if measuring its volume, weight, length and girth. Each one gleamed in the sunlight that was streaming through the window of the shop.

He had never seen gold nuggets. So it wasn't just a rumor. The sparkle in his eye was almost as brilliant as that of the gold itself, and his smile was as wide as his face would allow.

"It's really gold."

"Yes," replied the shopkeeper. "As big a covey of ladies as ever bared their buxom beauty and as big and beautiful as you're ever likely to see. They fill the streams. Nuggets as big as this, and bigger. Flakes wherever you look, as deep as the shovel can dig, and as fast as the streams can flow and deliver them up."

"Then, why aren't you there, too? Getting rich?"

"I was there, as you can see. I made my pile and sold my claim. I don't need to go back now. Sales have never been better. But, when miners stop buying guns, I'll go back, you can be sure of that."

Reef dropped the nuggets into the shopkeeper's hand, one by one, with long pauses and with great reluctance. The shopkeeper poured them into his fawnskin poke, one by one, with short pauses for maximum effect. He pulled the drawstring and dropped the poke into his inside coat pocket with an affectionate pat. He was more than happy to show them, and more than happy to talk about gold, because it only enhanced his reputation and increased his sales.

"I can see it in your face. You're going to go, aren't you?"

"Yes," replied Reef. "I have to. I'm a shipowner with landlocked ships. Finding gold is the easiest way to get back in business again."

"Landlocked ships? Those ships will never float again. Once those city dirt haulers fill the berths to make passageways and streets, the ships become permanent fixtures. They aren't going to go anywhere. Scavengers have stripped all the rigging to boot."

"That's true, but I can buy others that are still floating out in the bay waiting to be condemned."

"I understand. Well then, I think I have the things you'll be needing."

The shopkeeper brought a wooden case from underneath the counter. Reef picked up a Colt percussion pistol from its case and examined it front to back, top to bottom.

"Is this is the new Navy model?"

"Yes. No self-respecting jack or gold seeker was ever sorry he owned a Colt. Look at that workmanship."

Reef was a keen and eager appraiser of hardware of any kind, marine or otherwise. He studied it for a full minute, then raised it almost inch by inch to a full arm's length. He pulled the hammer back to half-cock, and then to full-cock. He aimed, then released the hammer with his thumb and a slight squeeze of the trigger. An aura of lust accompanied his appraisal.

"It's magnificent."

"Yes, it is. My last one for awhile."

"How much is it?"

"Twenty dollars."

Reef was shocked. The price was exorbitant and he protested.

"It's twelve back East."

The shop owner had a pat answer.

"No gold back East."

Reef was getting his first lesson in the economics of the gold rush. The shop owner continued.

"I can't keep 'em in stock. If you don't buy it, the next man that comes in the door will."

"All right, I'll take it. Let me see that Bowie."

The shopkeeper took a knife and sheath from the shelf behind him, turned, and handed them to Reef.

"Perfect for the Sierra hills. Feel the balance. Look at the engraving."

Reef squinted at it.

"A pan of gold nuggets? The gold seekers must like these. Are they getting rich? Tell me the truth."

"Adams & Co. loads a ship filled with gold for New York every week."

"Well," replied Reef, "at least Alvin Adams is getting rich, but what about the miners? Are they getting rich, too?"

The shopkeeper took the gold poke from his pocket. To remind Reef, he twirled it around his finger.

"You saw these. Gold sand. Gold pebbles. Gold flakes and gold nuggets. In the creeks. In the streams and in the rivers. Just lying there. Waiting to be taken."

Reef cradled the Bowie knife in his hand, balancing it back and forth, flipping it blade to grip, then grip to blade.

"I'll be needing this."

He pointed to a heavy post.

"May I?"

The shopkeeper nodded. Reef threw the knife at the post, sticking it with a deep cut into the wood. He walked to the post and jerked it to the side, attempting to snap it. The blade held fast. He jimmied the knife up-and-down until it was released from the post.

"I'll take it. How much for the Bowie and the Colt?"

"Twenty-two dollars."

"Do you have a chart?" asked Reef.

"Of course. One dollar more. I'll even mark the location of my claim. Stake one along the same creek and you'll come back a rich man."

The shopkeeper produced the chart and a holster, and placed them on the counter. Reef unfolded the chart and studied it as the shopkeeper penned in the claim's location.

" 'Stake a claim.' That's exactly what I plan to do."

Reef examined each one of his purchases, first the Colt, then the chart, then the Bowie. He folded the chart, returned the pistol to its case, and the knife to its sheath. He took a sailor's pea jacket from a stack on the counter, and tried it on. Too small. He tried on another. It fit. The price tag was three dollars. He handed it to the shopkeeper, who wrapped the items in heavy brown paper, and tied them with a strong faisal twine.

Reef took two ten-dollar bills from his billfold, a five-dollar gold coin and a dollar's worth of silver coins from his coin purse, and paid the shopkeeper. He picked up his bundle, left the shop, and closed the door behind him. One of Thai-Saing's two guards left his post to report Reef's whereabouts. The other followed Reef at a distance.

> *"September 30, 1853*
> *Received of R. Atherton, Boston*
>
> *1 Colt Navy, ser. #23,787 .... $20.00*
> *1 Bowie Knife 2.00*
> *1 Chart, Southern Mines 1.00*
> *1 Pea Jacket 3.00*
> *Total $26.00*
>
> *Paid in full w/ notes & specie."*
> *Receipt*
> *John Belding, Outfitter*

" ... On a hill, you get out and walk."

The activity at the California Stage Lines office was no less frenzied than it was along the wharf. Aspiring miners were pushing and shoving, and attempting to get in line for the available seats on any coach or mud wagon.

To a man, they were obsessed with getting to the gold country as fast as possible, as if the supply of gold dust in the streams would play out before they could even stake a claim.

A Concord coach, a driver, and an express messenger were waiting for the first sixteen passengers to board. The agent called out the ticket classes and accepted payment for passage.

"A first class ticket is five dollars. On a hill, you keep your seat. A second class ticket is four dollars. On a hill, you get out and walk."

The unruly passengers laughed. The humor eased the tension and they settled down, but soon they understood that the agent was serious.

"The third class ticket is three dollars. On a hill, you get off and push."

The men laughed again as the agent continued.

"The price of the ticket includes the ferry to Oakland. Boarding now. Step forward in line if you want a ticket."

Would-be passengers became animated again, and bumped one another to pay and board the coach. Reef did not reach for his coins. He had decided to conserve his money for necessities, and riding in a coach was not a necessity. Along with hundreds of others, he could walk to the Southern mines. He did not know what expenses he faced in the camps, so he passed up the ride, picked up his sea bag, and started walking in the direction of the Oakland ferry.

For five days and nights, Reef walked the wetlands, the flatlands, and into the foothills of the Sierras. Up and down the hills and along the dusty roads, he walked along with hundreds of other gold seekers.

When a mud-wagon or coach came from behind, it was always loaded with boisterous passengers, shouting obscenities, laughing, and waving. The pedestrians would respond with obscenities of their own. The shouting and the clatter of the horses' hooves, coupled with the hum of the wagon's wheels, would warn of an oncoming coach.

One of Thai-Saing's guards kept track of the roads that Reef traveled and the rivers that he crossed by drawing a map of each day's progress. The other guard posted the map to his master with any coach driver heading in the direction of San Francisco. The gratuity of fifty cents was enough to ensure that each map would be delivered.

"October 3, 1853 ... the gold seekers merely move to the side of the road without looking back. The coach passes them in a cloud of dust, laughter, and obscenities, at which time they move back onto the road and continue walking."

Newspaper article,
Alta California

"Any news from Syracuse?"

Finding a place to dig for gold was a simple matter. Like everyone else, Reef followed the endless line of men into the Sierra foothills. He would continue walking until he reached the creek marked on the chart by the shopkeeper. Finding tools and provisions was another matter. Reef was glad that the shopkeeper had told him to "fit out" in Sacramento.

Prices were exorbitant in San Francisco and higher in Sacramento, but thereafter the numerous towns and camps, with mercantiles and dry goods tents, were each more expensive than the last. Those that had any flour, salt beef, beans, utensils, and tools were charging ten to twenty times as much as in San Francisco. If one customer couldn't afford it, there was always someone standing behind him that could.

At the junction of each creek, the line of men split into two, with each man following the tributary of his choice. Miners were already in the creeks, picking, digging, and panning. The stakes of their claims were prominent, and tied with a rag pennant. A pistol on each man's waist, or on a tree stump nearby, attested to his willingness to protect his claim.

To Reef's surprise, the miners were pleasant to each other, with greetings for all, waving, taunts, and laughter. The newcomers meant less gold for those that were already here, which should make newcomers unwelcome, but the newcomers always brought something with them that was sorely missed and so desperately needed.

The newcomers brought news, and sometimes newspapers from back home, the miners' only link with their families. As Reef passed each miner, the miner's gaze followed him. It was an entreating gaze, a wishful stare, as if to say,

"Do we know each other?"

"Have we met?"

"Are you from home?"

The stare often continued until he passed the "high stakes" line, the imaginary line between the two stakes that marked the uphill perimeter of the miner's claim.

Occasionally, the miners quizzed the passersby with loud and audible questions, for anyone to hear, or no one to hear, and often without looking up, and without missing a stroke of their pick or shovel.

"I'm a miner from Caroliner."

"Any news from Syracuse?"

Far into the mountains, the man walking in front of Reef reached a plot of ground beyond the last high stakes, whereupon he dropped his bags of provisions and proceeded to stake it out. Reef continued to climb the hills far beyond that until he found the place marked on the chart. The two guards far behind him did the same, but now at an extended distance.

High upon the hill above him, Reef noticed a pale young man, and when their eyes met, the young man smiled and waved at the newcomer. Another miner had decided to go far beyond the nearest claim and get some privacy. Reef waved back, and continued to pace out his claim. That was more important than sinking his new pick and pan into the sands of the bubbling creek.

One of Thai-Saing's guards departed down the mountain to post the map. The other made preparations to spend the night and stay near his quarry.

"October 6, 1853 ... I wonder if all that I have traded, all that I have forsaken, is worth these pebbles of gold that I hold in my hand. Now, I know how Midas must have felt. It is late afternoon, it is very hot, and I am very lonely. ..."
Letter
Reef Atherton to Robin

"Pray louder. He don't look too good."

Reef sawed and nailed planks during the remaining autumn evenings, when the shadows had lengthened and gold in the bottom of the pan was no longer easy to see. A makeshift lean-to covered with a tarpaulin was remodeled into a dirt-floor shack with a tarpaulin roof and no windows and doors.

One month later, it had a door, a roof, and a tarpaulin floor. It slept one and housed his meager provisions, which he guarded jealously from a pair of mice that had adopted him.

Reef was resting in the shade of a pine tree when the storm clouds came and brought the rain. Reef got up and went inside the shack as the lightning and thunder warned him that it was about to pour. His supper fare was the standard hard tack, jerky, and cold beans, scooped from the frying pan while trying to avoid the leaks in the roof.

More lightning and thunder, and down came the rain. The mice came in from the rain, and he tossed them a piece of hardtack. The jerky was worse than the *old horse* on his father's ship, but it was better than nothing, so he saved it for himself. The mice began to nibble as he took the photograph from his chest pocket. He stared at it, then put it back. He folded his arms on his knees, put his head down, and wept.

He had risked everything and he had lost it all. He had declined a position in Larimore's bank. He had left his beloved Robin behind. He had traded it all. For what? To be living in this abject squalor. But he refused to give up, for he knew in his heart that someday all of his sacrifices would be worth the pain and the loneliness that he and Robin had endured.

He was in the stream early the following morning, panning and filtering through the sand. He was finding big nuggets, and he was feeling happy as he saw each new find gleaming in the bottom of a half-filled pan of sand and water. He tossed away many a pebble, and plenty of sand, but poured the pay dirt from the pan into a bulging gold poke. He arched his aching back and wiped his brow, then took a drink from the stream.

He saw the young miner upstream and waved. The miner waved back and walked down the hill toward him, shouting and competing with the babbling of the stream. Reef assumed that the miner was shouting a greeting, so he responded in kind.

"Good Morning."

"I've been watching you work your claim. Never had the chance to come by, though."

"You're a hard worker, yourself. Have you filed your claim yet?"

"Not yet. Have you?"

"No."

The young man extended his hand.

"I'm Charlie Boles. Springfield, Illinois."

"Reef Atherton. Boston."

"It'll be good having someone to talk to. The nights here get pretty lonely. I've got two newspapers, if you read."

"Yes, I can read. Thank you."

"I exchange them for new ones when I go into camp for supplies."

Reef was curious about the wisdom of going into camp.

"I've been told that someone will jump your claim if you leave it for too long."

"That's true. You have to be careful. I usually wait until early morning to go into camp, and I'm not gone more'n an hour or two."

"We can help each other watch the claims," offered Reef.

"Good and more important, get them filed."

"Yes. How are the diggings, by the way?"

"Best after a cloudburst. 'Course, half the mountain comes down on you at the same time. Took my shack with it the last time."

"Do you need some help rebuilding?"

"No, it's just about done. Come over after sundown, and I'll make some coffee."

"I'll be there. Thanks again."

Boles left. Reef watched him disappear, then went back to his panning.

Panning and picking. Picking and digging. Day after day. The heat goes away. Then the rains come. Then ice and snow abound, and the stream turns frigid. Then Reef finds out what part of each hour his feet can endure the frigid water before they become numb, and he can no longer stand. His boots are frozen and he can not remove them. He is tired and the day is almost over. Eat and sleep, then start a new day. Again and again, day after day.

He emptied his pan into his gold poke, picked up his hat, dried his feet, and put on his boots. He started back to the shack, which now had a wood floor, some planks of which covered his "big poke." Part way up the path, he paused, reacting to the two Chinamen outside the shack who were watching him approach. They drew their weapons at the same moment that he dropped his equipment and drew his.

An exchange of fire with them killed one, but Reef took a ball deep in the left shoulder near the collar bone, dropped to the ground, and lost his pistol. Lin Wu heard the shots and emerged from the shack with Reef's big poke under his arm.

Reef played possum until the two started running up the hill together. He reached for his boot, retrieved the Bowie, and threw the knife into the back of the nearest claim-jumper. His strength was spent and he passed out.

The claim-jumper dropped to his knees and grabbed Wu's belt. Wu turned. The dying man grabbed hold of the poke and pleaded for help with his eyes. When he would not release the poke, Wu kicked him in the groin to obtain possession. The man fell on his face and died. Wu surveyed the scene. He was satisfied that his mission had been accomplished.

Reef came to lying face down, bleeding, and unable to move. Boles had heard the shots and was running down the hill toward him. Appalled at what he saw, he verified that the two men were dead, then kneeled down beside his helpless friend.

"My God. What did they do to you?"

"They got me. Got my gold."

"Looks like you left your mark on a couple of 'em. How many were there?"

"Three."

"Lie still. I'm going to get you to a doctor."

"Just patch me up, and I'll walk to the camp. You can't leave your claim."

"Yes, I can. I filed it this morning. Lie still."

Boles knew that he had to stop the bleeding and get Reef down the mountain to a doctor. He wet his neckerchief in the frigid stream, and stuffed it inside Reef's shirt. He went into the shack, rummaged for another shirt, and tied it around Reef's arm and shoulder to hold the neckerchief in place.

He folded a tarpaulin around two stripped tree branches and eased Reef onto the makeshift stretcher. He retrieved Reef's pistol, and the knife from the corpse, and tossed them to Reef. Then, he lifted one end of the stretcher and started dragging his friend down the hill.

The Right Reverend Roland Pearson and his wife, Jeanne, lived about two miles down the mountain. Boles had listened to the preacher's fiery evangelical sermons at some of the camps, but he had attended the service more out of a desire to see a woman again than to be saved.

At least, the Pearsons had a wagon, and for a pinch or two, they would be inclined to transport Reef to the doctor. As Boles approached, he saw them working on the fence outside. When they heard Boles call out, they dropped their tools and rushed to assist him.

"Reverend. Can you give me a hand?"

"Praise Gawd, what happened?"

"It's my friend, Atherton. He's been shot. Gotta get him to Doc Trowbridge's. Two pinches for the use of your wagon."

"Jeanne, get bandages, blankets and pillows, and some water. I'll harness Violet," responded Pearson as he started out for the barn.

"Sure appreciate it, Reverend. He's passed out."

"Mr. Boles," said Jeanne, "For two pinches, we'll even say some special prayers, long, loud, and all the way down the mountain."

Jeanne went into the house and soon returned with bandages and blankets. Boles began bandaging Reef while Jeanne returned to the house for water and pillows. Reef came to and began to babble.

"Robin. Robin."

"Lie still, Reef. Nobody's robbin' you now. We're getting you to a doctor."

"Go back. Take gold back. Robin."

"No, Reef, no one's robbin' you. Lie still."

Jeanne returned with the pillows and water, then handed Boles another bandage. Pearson emerged from the barn with the wagon, stopped it, set the brakes, and lowered the gate. They lifted Reef and the stretcher into the wagon and climbed aboard. Pearson drove off, starting his prayer while Boles and Jeanne gave first aid and water to the bouncing patient.

"Lord, look down upon us. Praise Gawd, give us safe passage."

"Pray, Roland," interrupted Jeanne. "Pray louder. He don't look too good."

"Lord, befriend this sinner. Lord, we beseech Thee, save this man's life, for he is in Thy service, Lord, and much of Thy work he has left undone. Please don't let him die. Amen."

Pearson was hard put to improve upon that prayer at such a short notice. He was of the opinion that it was appropriate to repeat it often and aloud as the wagon rolled the bouncing foursome down the road.

The distance of ten or more miles to the doctor's house tested the preacher's praying power and found it in abundance. Pearson stopped the wagon at the doctor's house, still praying aloud. Boles jumped out and shouted toward the house.

"Hello, inside. Doc. Need help outside."

Pearson set the brake, jumped out, and helped Jeanne and Boles get a kicking and delirious patient to the edge of the wagon's gate. Madelaine and Beth Ellen Trowbridge heard the call and rushed out of the house to assist.

"Madelaine and Beth Ellen, Gawd help us, ladies. Grab a piece of him. He's a heavy one, he's kicking, and he weighs a metric ton," pleaded the preacher.

The three women, Boles, and Pearson hoisted the unconscious Reef out of the wagon, up the walkway, and inside the house. Madelaine grabbed the lace cloth and the candlesticks and removed them to make room for the others to spread Reef out on the dining table. Ellis Trowbridge entered from the back of the house as Beth Ellen offered him the first diagnosis.

"He's bleeding badly. He's delirious, he's thrashing, and he's kicking hard."

Trowbridge examined the wound.

"The artery is lacerated. We'll have to be careful. Get a compress, apply some pressure, and strap him down face up," responded Trowbridge.

Beth Ellen fetched the bandage and straps, applied the pressure to the wound, and Madelaine began preparations for the surgery. Boles, Pearson, and Jeanne strapped down his arms and legs, then his waist and hips. His murmuring grew louder. Some words were clear, but made no sense.

"... can't give up ... find it ... not a banker ... buy Robin ... Robin sings ..."

"Tie him down tighter, Reverend, or he'll kick the table apart," pleaded Beth Ellen.

"We're just about ready, Ellis," announced Madelaine.

She disinfected the clamps while Beth Ellen prepared the patient.

"Take his boots off, Mr. Boles. Quickly. Reverend, get the water. His shirt is stuck to his skin."

Beth Ellen reached for a pan, tampon, and towel. The Preacher brought hot water from the stove and poured it for her. She daubed the shirt around the wound with the steaming towel and tamponaded the wound. Reef screamed and kicked harder.

Dr. Trowbridge approached the melee with a bottle of whiskey, poured some into a pan of bandages and tampons, and handed the bottle to Boles. Boles paused, raised the bottle to the doctor, and then took a big swig. Despite the screaming and kicking, all present stopped what they were doing, turned, and looked at Boles.

"For good measure. Praise the Lord for this gathering and this noble endeavor."

Trowbridge nodded, reached for a clamp, then began to probe for the ball. Boles climbed on top of Reef. The preacher began to chant above the screams.

"Praise Gawd, give us the guidance. Steady our hands, and save this sinner."

Trowbridge shouted above the din.

"The ball's in there. It's at the ulnar. It's got to come out."

"... no banker ... pretty Robin ... Robin sings ... my claim ... can't sing ..."

Trowbridge probed deeper. Reef screamed louder. Trowbridge had had enough.

"Shut him up."

Madelaine twisted a wet towel, shoved it into Reef's mouth, and applied intense pressure. The doctor probed with the clamp, discarded it into the pan of disinfectant, and grabbed a smaller one. Reef emitted muffled screams and kicked with as much violence as his weakened condition could muster. Pearson continued his chant at full volume.

"Lord, save this man. Your work he has left undone. Save him, Lord."

Trowbridge struggled to locate the ball with the smaller clamp. Pearson's chanting wasn't helping.

"Shut him up, too."

"Softly, Roland. Pray softly," pleaded his wife.

"It's in there deep. Four or five inches. I've got it. It's coming ... it's coming ... got it."

Trowbridge dropped the clamp in the pan, retrieved the smashed ball, and tossed it to Boles.

"Here, Charlie. Your friend has a new watch fob. If he lives. Pressure on the wound. Be careful of the artery and sew him up. Quickly."

Reef was still. The doctor's wives produced large needles and thick thread, and began to sew. Boles returned to the floor. Pearson and his wife beamed and Trowbridge left the room to clean up. When he returned, he began to clean his instruments. Boles was cleaning Reef's Colt and Bowie. Trowbridge's wives were sponging and bandaging Reef, who was motionless and still delirious.

"... can't give up... Robin ... my gold ... Robin sings ... Caralina sings ...

At the mention of Caralina, the doctor froze, turned, and looked at Boles. The wives did not take notice.

"... buy Caralina ... buy Caralina ... can't give up ... my gold ..."

The doctor looked at Reef again, then at Boles. Boles shrugged and shook his head. They looked at each other, then at Reef. Trowbridge spoke in a hushed tone to Boles.

"See what you can find out when he wakes up."

Boles nodded. Reef continued to murmur and to dream. Boles emptied Reef's pockets on a table, next to the clean knife and pistol. He tossed a small gold poke to Pearson, who responded with enthusiasm.

"Praise Gawd, a soul with substance. You sustain us in our need, oh Lord, and we are grateful."

He wet his forefinger and thumb, then transferred two pinches of dust into his own gold poke. Beth Ellen approached with the family gold poke and turned to Madelaine. Madelaine extended three fingers. Pearson dropped his mouth, allowed her to take three dry lady-like pinches, then considered taking a third himself. Deciding against it, he pulled the drawstrings, tied them, and dropped the gold poke on the table. Boles smiled, then picked up the *Union* case and opened it.

"Ah. A dogtype. Look here. What a beauty. No wonder he works that claim so hard."

Pearson, Trowbridge, and their wives surrounded Boles to view the photograph. They looked at Reef and then at each other. The men smiled at each other in approval. The women pretended not to notice.

"December 11, 1853 ... Removed ball from left shoulder of Reef Atherton. Expect his arm will be paralyzed. If he lives."

Ellis Trowbridge
Journal of Surgery

"T welve is your number."

Sacramento was the hub of all modes of transportation and all markets in the summer of 1854. Rail, steamship, stage coaches, and wagon team drivers all converged on the town, supplying anxious miners with all of the food, liquor, and mining equipment that they needed and could afford, and dozens of items that they didn't need, couldn't afford, and bought anyway.

Anything that a miner wanted could be found on the docks near the rail terminal in Sacramento. As the first paddle wheeler docked each morning of the year with passengers eager to disembark, itinerant humbug peddlers on the docks uncovered their stores. Reef Atherton, thin and ashen, was one of them. His left arm was in a sling, which slowed him in getting his rather poor inventory of pistols, Bowies, and pocket scales uncovered and displayed for sale. Strength had returned to his arm, but the full use of his hand had not been restored. It hung from the wrist, about as ornamental and useful as an earlobe.

Eager gold seekers rushed off the boat and began bargaining with the peddlers, bumping and elbowing their way through the crowd. Reef held a pistol high above his head and showed it to the crowd. A gold seeker approached him, whereupon Reef almost forced it into the miner's hand and began his spiel.

"It's powerful, accurate, and reliable. You'll need one to protect your claim."

"How much is it?"

"Twenty-five dollars."

"Seems a bit high. They go for twelve back home."

Reef cashed the objection.

"They go for thirty dollars on J Street, and fifty in the camps. This is the best price in town."

The gold seeker was not happy, but he reached into his vest.

"All right, let's have it. Powder, caps, and balls included?"

"Five dollars more."

The buyer's mouth dropped.

"A dollar back home."

"No gold back home."

The gold miner winced, reached into his vest, and handed two gold coins to Reef.

"All right, let's have it."

Reef handed over the merchandise and the gold seeker stuffed the items into his satchel. Another man waited for the transaction to be completed and then approached Reef's stall.

"Mr. Atherton?"

"Yes?"

The speaker extended his right hand.

"I'm Sam Carson. I met you on the train from Boston to New York."

Reef shook hands and peered at the man. Indeed, it was Carson.

"So it is. So it is. It's good to see you again, Mr. Carson. What brings you all the way out here?"

"The same thing. Express and banking services for the gold camps."

Carson was dismayed by the condition of Reef's clothes, and the paucity of his inventory.

"Is this your livelihood now? I thought you were going to find your ships."

"I did, but the competition tore up my arm and ran me out. I'm still on the mend. Selling things that miners need is something I know and understand."

Carson thought a moment, then responded.

"We're looking for men. Reliable men. Willing to use a firearm should the occasion arise. You passed that test in Boston, Mr. Atherton. Would you consider coming to work for us?"

"Doing what?"

"We need another messenger. A hardware man. Someone to deal with outfitters and suppliers. Someone to order, stock, and deliver. Whatever we need in the camps."

"What kind of things do you need?"

"Right now, we need a beam balance that can weigh one ten-thousandth of an ounce."

Reef thought a moment.

"Howard & Davis has one. They're in Boston."

Carson picked up a pistol.

"And firearms. We need better firearms."

"These are Colts. The best. From New York."

"Come to San Francisco, Mr. Atherton. The pay is one hundred dollars a month. In gold."

Reef was surprised, thought a moment, and then looked beyond to the docks, the impertinent miners, and his competition.

"Not much of a future here, is there?"

Carson remained silent. He had made his point.

"All right, Mr. Carson. Where is your office? And when do you want me there?"

Carson extended his hand and Reef shook it.

"The Wells Fargo office. Montgomery Street, San Francisco. Day after tomorrow.

"I know the place. I'll be there."

Carson walked away. Reef watched him go, then turned to face an oncoming miner and raised another pistol above his head.

Reef was glad to leave Sacramento behind, and the many reminders that he was not cut out for mining. Perhaps Robin had been right; perhaps banking was the best path to wealth. Perhaps not. At least, he was glad to leave the heat of Sacramento for the cool air of San Francisco town.

Reef slung his sea bag over his right shoulder and jostled with the crowd getting off the Oakland Ferry. He walked through the noisy activity at the docks, and up Montgomery Street toward the banks. The banks, expresses, and stage lines were located almost next to each other: Adams & Co., Rhodes & Lusk, Freeman & Co., Page Bacon, and Wells Fargo & Co.

Horses and stage coaches were arriving and departing every establishment. Bank and express customers were conducting business in a feverish state of activity and urgency. Many men were on foot. Others were dismounting and mounting horses, or getting in and out of mud wagons for hire. Reef stood in front of the California Stage Co., next to the Wells Fargo office, and watched the drama play. Boys, eight and ten years of age, were vying for pennies from customers to hitch, water, and watch their horses while they were inside the offices.

Reef took notice of one small chap, no more than five years old, who was trying to compete, but was woefully outclassed by the older boys. Carson was bidding goodbye to a customer. He closed the coach door, waved to the driver for the coach to depart, and then turned to see Reef.

"Good Morning, Mr. Atherton. Welcome to San Francisco."

"Thank you. What's going on here?"

"They're local urchins. They make a few pennies a day watering horses up and down the street."

Another stage coach was rumbling down the street. The youngster, bent upon beating a ten-year old to a customer, failed to see the coach. Reef dropped his bag, lunged for the boy with his good arm, and pulled him out of the path of the oncoming horses. He waved his lame arm and yelled to scare the lead horses.

The tactic worked enough to alter the path of the lead horses and the swings, but near-wheeler horse clipped him and knocked the two into the street. They were dirtied but safe, coming to rest at the foot of a shy, well-dressed Chinaman and his entourage. Reef ignored them and the other onlookers, got up, and brushed off the little boy.

"Hey, little fellow, you have to be more careful. You can get killed for not looking."

The boy was crying and scared.

"I'm sorry. I just wanted a penny."

"What's your name?"

"J.J."

Carson was glad to see that both were unhurt.

"Are you both still in one piece?"

"I think so. That was close, though."

"I'd hate to lose you on your first day. You, too, little jack."

J.J. was still crying, but spunky enough to correct the man.

"I'm J.J."

Carson was amused.

"Fine, J.J., but we're going to have to keep you out of the street. How would you like to work for Wells Fargo?"

J.J. was composing himself, but was leery of Carson.

"I guess so."

Carson picked up J.J. and put him on the back of a white horse that was hitched in front of the office.

"This is Strawberry. Can you feed and water him for us?"

J.J. was warming up to his new status.

"Yes."

"And we have four others. When the messengers bring them in, you'll have to care for them, too. Can you do that?"

"Yes, mister."

"Call me Mister Sam. That's five horses total, so I'll pay you five pennies a day."

J.J. beamed. This was a fortune to him.

"Yes sir, Mister Sam."

"Now, you take care of my horses. This is Mr. Atherton. When you're not busy in the stable, you can help him. And stay out of the street."

J.J. grinned at both men.

"Yes, Mister Sam. Thank you, Mister Affermin."

Reef laughed, took J.J. off the horse, and put him on the sidewalk.

"Just call me Mister Reef."

The two men turned away from the boy and entered the office. The boy reached for Reef's hand, followed them inside, and then disappeared to explore the office and stable. Reef put his bag down and took off his coat and hat. Carson hung them on a coat rack.

"He's one of the smaller ones. Has a tendency to get pushed around by the older boys."

"That was a fine thing you did."

Carson sat at a desk, opened a ledger, took a quill pen, and dipped it into an ink well.

"It wasn't charity. We need a stable boy, and our horses are gentle. He's in no danger here, and he'll earn every penny. So will you. We all do."

Carson made an entry in the ledger.

"J.J. Travis. Stable boy. Five cents a day."

Carson made another entry.

"Reef Atherton. Messenger number twelve. $100 dollars a month, payable in gold."

"Twelve?"

"Carl Hodges is number ten. Glenn Sutton is eleven. Twelve is your number. Twelve is your signature and your seal on all company business. You now represent the company. You can deliver and receive gold dust, paper, and specie for deposits and express forwarding to this office and our agents. Are you ready to go to work?"

"Yes."

Carson reached in the drawer and took out a paper list.

"Fine. Here's a list of what our offices need. Take a company horse and wagon to the camps to deliver the supplies and bring back the gold dust. J.J. can help you around town. See me for anything over $100, and thanks again for joining us."

Carson offered his hand. Reef shook it and studied the list.

"Thank you. The beam balance you asked me about will cost about two hundred dollars."

"Get it. Company letterheads and franks are in these drawers. You can use this desk. Any questions?"

"No, not at the moment."

Carson walked away. Reef took off his coat, sat at the desk, rummaged for an order form and envelope, and began writing. J.J. returned to the office and sat down opposite Reef.

"J.J., where can I post a letter?"

J.J. glanced around and then pointed to a red letter box on the wall across the room.

"Over there."

"Will you post this for me?"

"What is it?"

"I'm buying a beam balance."

"What's that?"

"It's something that can weigh the freckles on your nose."

Reef pinched J.J.'s nose and J.J. giggled. Reef folded and inserted the letter into the stamped envelope, sealed it, and handed it to J.J.

"Now, off with you. Post this and come back. We have some places to go."

J.J. took the letter, posted it, and the two left the office.

"June 27, 1854 ... Reef Atherton appt'd Msgr. 12, salary of $100.00 per month, payable in gold."
    Journal Entry
    Wells Fargo & Co. Express

"I was planning on buying her ..."

J.J. followed Reef a few doors down the street and into a gunsmith's shop. Tong Wen-How observed their movements without concern and waited for them to reappear. Reef and the boy transacted their business with the gunsmith for about thirty minutes. Wen-How waited with his companions. Reef bid goodbye to the gunsmith and walked toward a nearby harness shop. Again, Reef and J.J. spent a considerable period of time in the shop, the passage of which did not concern Wen-How. As J.J. and Reef emerged from the harness shop, the Chinaman approached them. Reef was apprehensive. His recent experience with the members of that race had left him a bit gun-shy. Wen-How addressed Reef.

"Please excuse me. Mr. Wells Fargo?"

"I beg your pardon?"

"Mr. Wells Fargo, I have been watching you. My name is Tong Wen-How."

"You've been watching me?"

"Yes. That is not polite, is it? Please accept my apologies."

"Well, no harm done, but why?"

"I have much gold that needs safe-keeping. I am asking that Wells Fargo keep it for me."

"I don't understand."

"My people think that bad spirits live in the dwellings of Adams and Page Bacon. We like the spirits that dwell with Wells Fargo."

"To be honest with you, so do I."

Wen-How removed a large gold poke from his coat and handed it to Reef.

"We give our gold to Wells Fargo. Place this in the name of Tong Wen-How. Tomorrow, more of us will bring gold into your dwelling for safekeeping.

Wen-How bowed, turned, and started to walk away. Reef was surprised.

"Wait. Don't you want a receipt?"

Wen-How stopped, turned, smiled, and bowed again.

"A receipt is not necessary. You risked your life to save this urchin from great harm. You covet life, not gold."

He bowed again, turned, and walked away, leaving Reef to resolve his surprise and take charge and due regard of his newest responsibility. He and J.J. returned to the bank to deposit the gold.

The day was filled with similar calls on suppliers, discussions, and negotiations for filling orders for the company offices. Reef called it quits around eight in the evening, stood up from his desk, and stretched. He retrieved his hat, coat, and bag. He bid Carson good day, and left the office. J.J. was right behind him and Reef took his hand.

"J.J., we had a full day, didn't we?"

"Yes, Mr. Reef."

"I'll take you home, now, and then go find a place to stay. Where do you live?"

"With my Mimi. Come home and stay with me, Mr. Reef. Please. Please."

"Well, I'll take you home, anyway. Maybe your Mimi knows a good rooming house."

They walked down the street. One merchant pretended to sweep J.J. away with a broom, and another gave him a small sack of food to take home. J.J. seemed to be well known along the streets of San Francisco town.

The San Francisco & Oakland Ferry was docking as J.J. steered Reef toward the terminal. The deckhands worked with the dockers to tie up and position the gangplank. Caralina was watching them, waiting to entice some of the disembarking passengers. Charlie Boles, well dressed with hat and cane, walked off the ferry as Reef and J.J. approached. They greeted each other with warm handshakes.

"Reef. You're still alive."

"Charlie. You're looking well yourself, and prosperous to boot."

"Sold my claim and lookin' to buy another. It's good to see you back in one piece, again. How's the arm?"

"It's mending just fine. Those Trowbridge ladies sew a fine stitch. Thanks for what you did."

"Too bad about your claim, though. Did you ever go back to it?"

"No. Too rough on these old bones. I found work here in town. This little fellow is my --"

The sight of Caralina interrupted Reef's thought, and he called to her.

"Caralina."

At the sound of her name, Boles' interest was awakened, but he remained silent as Reef began walking toward the girl and called her name again.

The noise of the steamer and the crowds drowned out his call. Caralina appeared not to notice and disappeared among the passengers. Boles wanted more information about the girl, the one that Doctor Trowbridge had sent him to find.

"Who is she?"

"A street urchin. An orphan, I think. A sing-song girl, bonded to a Chinaman. I saw her down at the docks, once. I was planning on buying her before his men attacked me. They're the ones who stole my gold."

"You want to buy her?"

"Buy her bond. They're all for sale, you know. All those girls."

"So that's what the doctor has in mind," reasoned Boles.

"Trowbridge?"

"Yes. He sent me to find out about her. He wants to buy her, too. That's all I know."

Reef gazed after the girl with sadness in his face. Boles saw that there was nothing more to gain by quizzing Reef, so he changed the subject.

"Well, Reef, I'm staying at the Barclay Hotel for a few days. Do stop in and have a drink and dinner with me. For old times sake."

"I'll do that, Charlie. If you need me, I work at the Wells Fargo office on Montgomery. So, you say Dr. Trowbridge wants to buy her, too?"

"Yes, that's what he says."

"That's interesting. All right, Charlie, we'll talk about this later. I have to take this little fellow home."

They shook hands and parted company. J.J. tugged at Reef's sleeve, pulling him away from the revenue traffic of pedestrians and carriages. Toward the back of the ferry, a stoker was supervising some men loading cords of wood into the ferry's hopper chute. The sound of the boilers was deafening, joining a chorus of two long howls of the whistle.

Anita was nearing the ferry, pulling her wagon behind her. She saw J.J. get excited, break free of Reef, and run over to the ferry, waving and yelling above the roar.

"Daddy Al. Daddy Al."

The stoker turned, smiled, then laughed and waved.

"Aha, J.J. How's my favorite little boy?"

"Fine, Daddy Al. Daddy Al, this is Mr. Reef. He wants to come and live with us."

Reef laughed and yelled back, modifying the request.

"Do you know of a good room and board?"

"How does fifty cents a day sound? One week in advance and the best meals you'll find anywhere in town?"

"Sounds just fine to me. I'll take it."

Anita remembered Reef at once. She ignored him. She left her wagon, walked up to the ferry, and handed the stoker a lunch pail and a water container. She turned to give Reef his first glimpse of her. She was crestfallen. Reef did not remember her. With mischievous delight in her intent to punish him, she pursued her quarry.

"Aren't you the man who -- "

Daddy Al pointed to her and yelled at Reef while looking toward the bridge to get any last minute orders from the captain.

"Give the money to my daughter, and she'll show you the way home."

Daddy Al looked back, waved, and went below. The whistle howled three times, loud and long. Crewmen pushed away from the dock with grappling poles and the ferry moved forward. Reef dug into his pocket for the $3.50 and handed it to Anita. Anita took the money, then shouted over the noise of the departing ferry.

"I'm Anita. What's your name?"

"Reef Atherton."

"What?"

"Reef. Reef Atherton."

"Reef? Like in the ocean?"

"Yes. Like in the ocean."

Anita nodded. She started to say something, but quit trying to talk above the station noise. She retrieved her wagon and motioned for Reef to follow her up Market Street with J.J. in tow. She looked behind her and saw that J.J. was lagging behind, but she did not see Caralina following at a distance.

"Come on J.J. Catch up with us."

"Go slower, Annie."

Reef understood J.J.'s plea.

"Your little brother must be very tired. He's been showing me around all day long. I'll carry him the rest of the way."

Anita was startled that Reef had called J.J. her brother. He didn't know. She started to correct him, then hesitated. She remained silent. Reef handed his bag, hat, and the sack of food to Anita, and put J.J. on his shoulders.

She put the things in the wagon, and they continued to walk side by side. When he looked away, up the street, or in a shop window, she took each opportunity to drink in his presence and his nearness. She was careful to look away whenever he looked at her, and she pondered her options.

How brazen and improper of me to let him think that I have any interest in him whatever. Older men have reputations for taking advantage of young girls that are curious and show too much interest. However, when he speaks to me, it is only polite to face him and respond, and I will do so at every opportunity. Oh, please say something.

While Anita played out her fantasy, Caralina contrived to approach Reef from behind and embrace him. He was the one. The attractive one. Old, to be sure, but still attractive enough. It would be fun to entice this handsome stranger, and then to be held fast, shaken, and scolded so warmly in return.

"Can I sing for you mister? A song of love for five pinches?"

Anita awakened from her dreamland with an apprehensive search for Lin Thai-Saing. Darn Caralina anyway. She could have any man she wanted. Why did she have to pick on her Reef? Anita resolved herself to the inevitable and took a tighter grip on her wagon. She moved it away from Reef and Caralina, a half dozen paces behind them, and as far as the boardwalk would allow between them. Reef was upset.

"It's you. You're still here. You're too young for this."

"Grown up enough for you. Bet you another pinch you'll agree. Another pinch says that you'll be singing to me by tomorrow morning."

Reef angered. He deposited J.J. on the ground, then grabbed Caralina and shook her.

"Stop this. Have you no place to go? Doesn't anyone take care of you? Why don't you stop doing this?"

Caralina was shaken from her normal routine. He was not being gentle this time. What did it take to get this old coot interested in her? She pretended to be frightened, and tried to get away, breaking into crocodile tears.

"I do the best I can, mister. I have to eat. I don't have it easy like you."

"What about your father? Doesn't he feed you? Doesn't he take care of you?"

The mention of her beloved father angered the girl, and she returned Reef's fury in like kind, a painful response that she had learned to give her self-righteous inquisitors.

"Well, I'm here, aren't I?"

Then she was sorry. He had tried to rescue her and Wu had beaten him senseless. He had been kind to her, and he did not deserve her disrespect. Her eyes began to moisten against her will. She broke free and ran toward Lin Thai-Saing, Wu, and two other sing-song girls who were working the street with her. Anita observed the scene in sadness, walked up to Reef, and took his arm in comfort. They walked the rest of the way in silence.

Anita's mother was paring apples on the porch of their little house when she caught sight of Reef,

Anita, and J.J. She greeted them with a cheerful laugh.

"Hello, Annie. Who's your friend? A bill collector?"

"A payin' customer, Mimi. This is Mr. Reef Atherton. He's going to room and board with us."

"Welcome to our home, Mr. Atherton. I'll let Annie show you the room."

"Thank you, Mrs. --"

"Travis, but you can call me Mimi like everyone else."

"Fine, Mimi. Thank you. Please call me Reef."

"Reef. Good name for a man. Strong-sounding. Like a rock."

"Yes, Ma'am. A rock."

Anita seized the golden opportunity to make sport of him. Besides, it would serve him right to be punished for forgetting her.

"C'mon, Strong-like-a-rock Reef Atherton. I'll show you the room. You'll love the mattress. It's strong, too, and hard as a rock."

"Anita, watch what you say. You'll scare him off."

Reef laughed. He was going to enjoy his stay with this family. This girl had spunk, sparkle, and a good sense of humor, something of which his life had been devoid in the past few months. He followed the girl inside. Anita lead Reef to a bedroom door, but placed her back to it, blocking his entrance. With her hands behind her and her chin and shoulders erect, she felt sure that she presented her best front to him.

"This'll be your room. I'll have to clean it a bit and make the bed."

"Oh, it's fine the way it is. Let me see my new home."

"Nope. I'll clean it first, but I will take your coat, sir. You sit at the table, and I'll serve up some supper."

Reef obeyed, and handed Anita his coat. As she folded it over her arm, Robin's photograph almost dropped to the floor, but Anita grabbed it just in time.

"Ohhh. What's this? Ooo-ee. It's a dogtype. Can I see it? Please?"

"Go ahead. Open it."

"Ohhh. She's beautiful. Mimi. Come and see. Reef has a sweetheart."

Reef started to correct the girl.

"No, not exactly, she's --"

Mimi's voice interrupted him.

"A sweetheart?"

Anita gazed at the beautiful face in the photograph. She saw her own face reflected by the mirrored surface, and began wiping her own face, and fussing with her hair and dress. Reef had not seen a woman primp in a long time, and he enjoyed watching her. Anita answered her mother.

"A picture. Reef's sweetheart. She's so ... beautiful."

Mimi came indoors and crossed the room to them.

"Let's see. Ohhh. She is beautiful. What's her name?"

Reef abandoned any thought of revealing his marriage. He preferred to wait for a better and more appropriate time. No need to complicate things now.

"Robin, thank you."

Appraising her competition, Anita now regretted initiating the incident. She closed the case, put it in the coat pocket, and handed the coat to Reef.

"Well. Let's have some supper."

Reef was relieved that the incident was over.

"Yes. Supper."

They went to the table. Reef deposited his coat on the chair, washed and dried his hands at the sink, and sat down. Mimi and Anita set the table and served the supper.

"June 27, 1854 ... It was ten o'clock before we fed Mr. Atherton. His sweetheart is so pretty. What can I do to make him forget her?"

Diary of Anita Travis

" ... Guard a treasure box with a bird gun?"

On vacant property in the hills at the end of Market Street, Reef tacked a two-foot square of heavy brown paper to an abandoned shed. He picked up a shot gun, poured powder and a cloth wad down one of the barrels, took the ramrod, and rammed them home. Then, he poured shot and another wad down the barrel and rammed them. He stowed the ramrod, and placed a percussion cap on the nipple of the loaded barrel. The sun was beginning to herald the new day and he felt a sense of accomplishment.

As he paced off twenty feet from the target, Carl Hodges and Glenn Sutton approached. Reef exchanged greetings with them.

"Good morning, Mr. Hodges, Mr. Sutton."

"Mr. Atherton."

Sutton went right to the point.

"What's this all about?"

"I'm thinking of buying these for you, and I want to see what you think of them."

Hodges was appalled by what he saw.

"A bird gun?"

Sutton caught the implication.

"You want us to guard a treasure box with a bird gun?"

Reef was not pleased with their reaction.

"Just wait. Give it a fair chance."

"All right, let's see it."

All three men turned to face the shed. Reef rested the gun on his left forearm, cocked the hammer behind the load, and lifted the gun to his shoulder. The two messengers looked at each other, then looked at the shed.

Reef took aim, and fired. His aim was good. A tight pattern of holes was blown into the center of the paper. Hodges and Sutton looked at each other. They looked back at the paper. Sutton was the first to speak.

"Yes, that's what a bird gun does, all right."

"I think this needs more thought, Atherton."

The two messengers shook their heads, turned, and walked away. Reef was motionless, and continued to look at the paper. He was not pleased with their reaction, or with the results of his experiment.

Reef walked down to the house, ate breakfast, took J.J. by the hand, and proceeded to the gunsmith's shop. He asked the owner to examine the shot gun, with the view of modifying it to widen the pattern in the paper.

"We're not concerned with aiming. We just want to point, shoot, and hit something. Whatever we hit will show us where to point for the second shot."

"You want to hit something and you're not going to aim? That's asking for a lot, isn't it?"

"We just want to point. Point in the general direction."

"Well, I can cut a few inches off the barrels and the rod, but that's going to ruin a fine gun and people will laugh at you."

"I'll risk it. Go ahead and cut off the barrels. What else can you do?"

The gunsmith reached below the counter and brought up some bird shot samples.

"How about a larger size of shot?"

Reef selected a large sample.

"Let's try this one."

"All right. Come back day after tomorrow."

"Day after tomorrow. Good. Come, J.J."

Reef left the shot gun, picked up the paper target, and walked out of the shop with the boy.

Anita, Mimi, Daddy Al, and J.J. were gathered around the table after supper, and laughed as Reef related the story and exhibited the shot-riddled paper.

"This was my big chance to show the messengers my superior skill at purchasing firearms for the company."

Anita came to him and took the paper.

"But I don't understand. You hit it, didn't you?"

"Yes, but a highwayman can see where I'm pointing and duck."

J.J. was eager to participate in the frolic.

"Quack, quack. Quack, quack."

"Not that kind of duck, J.J.," responded Anita.

She approached Reef.

"This kind."

Anita put her hands on top of Reef's head, and pulled it forward and downward, level with hers. He pretended to pout, ducked his head, and everyone laughed. She took the riddled paper, began folding it into a paper hat, and mimicked an official's voice.

"Well, Mr. Atherton, here at Wells Fargo, we appreciate your valiant efforts on our behalf. Therefore, we award you this as a token of our deep appreciation."

She put the paper hat on his head Napoleon-wise. They all laughed. Anita reached forward, and gave Reef a tender hug. Other than Caralina, he had not been near a girl since he had bid Robin goodbye. Anita's attention, her warmth, and her tenderness aroused unmistakable feelings of desire within him. He denied these feelings and admonished himself.

I feel guilty. But I didn't do anything. She hugged me. I am married. I will not allow myself to enjoy or pursue any such feelings for this girl, ever. That whole idea would be ridiculous anyway, because I am old enough to be her father. Besides, she was just being polite in hugging me, like including me as one of the family. And besides, she hugged everyone else, too. Didn't she?

His embarrassment was evident, to the delight of the others applauding Anita's gesture. He returned the hug, still showing his embarrassment.

"July 1, 1854 ... He is fun to hug because his face gets so red. I will do it again soon. And again, if he will let me."
                    Diary of Anita Travis

"Now write your name on it."

Reef was happy to leave the office and travel. The horselaughs about the shot gun incident had subsided, but the sting of failure still pierced his pride. A peaceful ride on the night steamer to Sacramento deposited him and his crates on the dock at sunrise, a few hundred feet from the company's office. A wagon and horse were provided by the agent, along with assistance in loading the crates and directions to Auburn.

Reef took his time, cradled his precious shipment on a bed of excelsior and blankets, and nursed it into Auburn by sundown and stopped at the company office. He had no intention of giving the agent any fuel to fire up another company joke at his expense. Johnson was a young agent, with a healthy sense of humor who lost no time attacking the funny bone, once the amenities had been exchanged. Johnson viewed the crates in the wagon, looked at Reef and grinned.

"Did you bring me some bird guns, Mr. Atherton?"

"Not this trip, sonny, but I'll keep you in mind."

Reef and Johnson spent most of the evening setting up the beam balance. Johnson was intrigued. The pans were almost as big as those of the miners, and the beam was a full three feet wide. He had never been able to weigh a poke of gold down to one thousandth of a grain, and could not fathom such a massive machine being able to do so. His skepticism increased as the final parts were put into place, and began rubbing his chin and shaking his head. Reef was finished with the assembly and it was time for him to perform.

"Now watch this. Put a blank waybill on one pan and balance it with grain weights."

Johnson complied, taking a box of grain weights, and watching the pointer move toward zero as he dropped weights into the balance pan. At zero, he reached for the lever and stopped the pans. Reef pointed to the paper.

"Now write your name on it."

Johnson was curious. His name? What has that to do with anything? He took the paper from the pan, signed it with a pencil, and then placed the waybill back on the pan. Reef responded.

"Now, let them go."

Johnson was dubious. He looked at Reef. He looked at his signature. He reached for the lever. They looked at each other. Reef nodded. Johnson released the pans and stared at the pointer. Nothing happened. They waited. Then it happened. The pointer crept in the direction of the paper. Johnson's eyes widened, looking at one pan, then the other, then back to the first, and then at Reef. He repeated the cycle. He had lost the bet. He fumbled for a dollar and flipped it to Reef.

"All right, Mister Atherton, here's your dollar. I didn't think you could do it."

Reef smiled in satisfaction, looked at the agent, and folded his arms. He needed a victory, and this was as good as any.

Daddy Al Travis was stoking the ferry the next night when Reef returned to San Francisco and walked up Market Street to his adopted home for supper. Mimi, J.J., and Anita examined the waybill with Johnson's signature as Reef sat at the table and related the event to them. Anita needed an explanation.

"I don't understand. Why do you weigh pencil markings?"

Reef laughed.

"We don't. It was just a test, a demonstration, but we could do it if we had to."

Anita grinned, shook her head, folded the waybill into a long feather, and mimicked an official.

"Well, in that case, Mr. Atherton, for weighing Wells Fargo pencil scratches, we feel that you deserve a feather in your cap."

She retrieved the paper hat from a drawer, stuck the paper feather in it, and put the hat sideways on Reef's head. They all laughed. She sat on his lap and gave him a prolonged wet kiss on the cheek that ended with her dry lips brushing all the way to his for a hurried press, after which she parted their union. Not really a *capital K* kind of kiss, but enough of her taste to stimulate his interest.

His interest was indeed stimulated. Again. Again, he admonished himself.

I already went over this. There is nothing between us, and she is just being friendly and polite.

His embarrassment was evident once again, and the others applauded the gesture. He held her tightly for only one precious moment, consumed her aroma, then released her and looked at Mimi, who was smiling in approval while J.J. giggled.

"July 5, 1854 ... Rec'd Howard & Davis gold scales, $200."
> *Entry in the Property Book*
> *Wells Fargo & Co.*
> *Auburn, Cala.*

"I want her, Charlie. And, I want her alive."

Charlie Boles finished his dessert, complimented the Trowbridge wives for their cooking and hospitality, and accepted the doctor's invitation to depart for the living room. The wives attended to the table and the dishes while the doctor entertained their guest.

"I want to thank you for coming tonight, Charlie."

He lowered his voice and continued.

"What news have you?"

"I was in San Francisco and ran into Reef down at the ferry."

"How is he doing?"

"Fine, from all appearances, except for a weak hand. He works for Wells Fargo, now."

"Good. What did he have to say?"

"Hold onto your hat. We saw Caralina. He called to her, but she lost us in the crowd."

"Caralina. Did you get a look at her?"

"Yes. A pretty thing. I had dinner with Reef a few days ago. She propositioned him, you know."

"And?"

"He throttled her good and she ran off. That happened down at the docks."

"Can you find her again?"

"I think so. She works for a Chinaman down there."

"Yes, the docks. That's where I first saw her. We had just arrived in San Francisco."

Trowbridge looked at Boles, reached for his money pouch, then spoke to him in confidence.

"I lost her in the crowd, too, and I couldn't find her. I want her, Charlie. I want her. Go find her for me. Go directly to the Chinaman and negotiate with him. Here's one hundred dollars for your expenses. I'll pay you two hundred more when we have her."

This should be interesting. Reef said that he wanted to buy her, too, but Trowbridge was willing to pay Boles to set it up. Boles took the money.

"I'll write when I find her."

"Good, but be cautious. Sometimes our letters arrive opened. Call her *surgical supplies*, and call the Chinaman the *supplier*. And divide the money amounts by ten."

"All right, doctor. I'll get her for you, but why don't you just take him to court? The Chinese have no legal standing against us. He'll lose."

"He might kill her. Or sell her out of spite and spirit her away. I want her, Charlie. And, I want her alive."

"All right, doctor."

Beth Ellen passed silently by the doorway and overheard her husband. Her curiosity got the better of her and she stopped to listen.

"Thank you, Charlie. Are you nervous about this?"

"Yes, doctor, I suppose. A bit."

"Charlie."

"Yes, doctor?"

"Don't be so nervous. And please call me *Ellis*."

"Why, thank you doctor. I mean, Ellis. I'll settle down. I'll be all right, and I'll see to this right away."

"This will take you away from your claim."

"I filed it and sold it to the mining company. I don't have a claim for now. Maybe I'll get another. After we buy Caralina."

Boles got up, the two shook hands, and Boles took his leave. Beth Ellen waited until Boles had gone, then entered, and inquired of her husband with a tremor in her voice.

"Buy Caralina? That little girl at the docks? You're going to buy her, Ellis?"

"Be still about this, woman. Not a word to anyone. Not even to Madelaine."

Beth Ellen was not pleased, and she was cowed by her husband, but she was a loyal wife. She left the room. Trowbridge was troubled at her eavesdropping. The fewer that knew about this, the better.

"July 7, 1854 ... Ten dollars paid to Charlie Boles for surgical supplies."
                    Ellis Trowbridge
                    Money Record Book

"Give me a gun that can do the job"

Early morning sunrise found Reef tacking another sheet of brown paper to the abandoned shed in the vacant lot at the end of Market Street. Reef picked up the shot gun and finished loading both barrels, now only twenty inches long. Hodges and Sutton approached, jovial and laughing. Reef waited for them with his greeting.

"Carl, Glenn."

Hodges responded.

"Reef."

"I think you'll see an improvement this morning."

"Another bird gun?"

"I have some bigger shot and I shortened the barrels. You'll see an improvement."

All three faced the shed. The two messengers looked at each other, then looked back at the shed. Reef took aim, and fired. The shot blew a much wider pattern of holes, perforating the entire target. The three men did not move. The two messengers looked at each other, then looked back at the paper. Sutton made an observation.

"Yep. That's an improvement, all right, but you have to do it when you're on top of a coach. Like this. Grab his coat, Carl."

The two men began rocking Reef forward and backward, side to side, simulating the bounce and sway of a coach. Sutton made his point.

"Highwayman ahead, Atherton. Shoot him."

Reef triggered the remaining shot. It missed both the paper target and the shed. Sutton patted Reef on the back, and the messengers turned and walked away. Reef continued to stare at the paper.

Reef argued at length with the gunsmith later that day about the riddled paper and the gun.

"The pattern is too tight, and the gun is too heavy. We have to be able to swing it fast, from one side to the other."

"Swing it? Mister, you're going to kill someone that way."

"That's the general idea."

"What? Who?"

"Highwaymen. From a moving coach. Give me a gun that can do the job."

The gunsmith was perplexed. He left the room, then returned a moment later with much larger shot samples. Reef chose the largest. The gunsmith indicated another barrel cut. Reef pointed to the shortest possible cut. The gunsmith shook his head, but agreed at Reef's insistence. Reef left the gun and retrieved the paper target.

After supper, Anita and J.J. seated themselves in anticipation of Reef's latest exhibit. Reef unfolded the riddled paper. They all laughed, and J.J. fetched the paper hat and feather. With Mimi and Daddy Al down at the ferry, Anita decided to make the best of this opportunity.

"This is an improvement? Or a failure? Which?"

"Oh, no, it's an improvement."

"What's it mean?"

"This is the chest of an unlucky highwayman."

"Oh. That's ghoulish. Is this what you do all day?"

They laughed. Anita opened Reef's coat, stuffed a corner of the paper target in his collar and one in each coat sleeve. She pretended embarrassment while Reef pretended gallantry and stuffed the fourth corner into his pants. J.J. handed the paper hat with the paper feather to Reef, who surrendered and put it on. They laughed again. Reef and Anita looked at each other. They were silent. Anita came to him, put her arms around his neck and hugged him.

J.J. was still and quiet, as he watched her kiss Reef on the mouth. Not a brazen kiss, not a wanton kiss, but a sweet kiss, warm, and wet enough to make him remember that he had been kissed. Embarrassed, she made a hasty retreat to her room, just as he began to return her kiss. J.J. clapped his hands and giggled.

> *"July 15, 1854 ... I kissed him today and I ran, but before I closed the door, I turned and looked back at him. His face was bright red!"*
>
> *Diary of Anita Travis*

"If I survive, you get paid."

The carpenter was doing his best to prove the merits of the trunk, but Reef was not pleased. He fumbled with an iron strap and a trunk hinge on the counter. He tapped them on the wooden trunk.

"No, you've got to do better. Your trunks are made out of pine. They wear away and they break open. I need something much stronger. Something that you can, say, roll off of Telegraph Hill."

"Roll off of Telegraph Hill? Mister, No trunk'll survive a roll off of Telegraph Hill."

"Well, that's what I want. Reinforce it with these if you have to. Do whatever it takes."

"Iron straps?"

"Yes. Top, bottom, and sides. With heavy iron hinges."

"That'll cost more money."

"Just build one. Let me know when it's done. I'll test it myself."

"You'll test it? How?"

"I'll get in it. You roll it off of Telegraph Hill. If I survive, you get paid."

The carpenter raised his eyes to the ceiling, but he registered his agreement and shook hands with Reef. Reef turned to depart, then returned with the iron strap, deposited it in the carpenter's hand, and made good his exit.

When Reef met the carpenter on Telegraph Hill, ships were coming into the bay in a stream, spotting the tower above him, firing one cannon shot, and telegraphing cargo manifests to the brokers in the tower. Brokers were reading the telegraph signals, making notes and passing them to boys to run the news into town.

The carpenter unloaded the trunk from a wagon and positioned it at the edge of a steep incline. One or two of the brokers were curious enough to interrupt their business and watch. Reef got in, wrapped a horse blanket around his head and back, and hunched down. The carpenter closed and locked the lid. The brokers were speechless, and tugged at the arms of others to witness the spectacle.

The carpenter rolled the trunk off the hill. The brokers were astounded. The trunk careened, bounced, crashed, and rolled a few hundred feet, with the carpenter in pursuit. At the bottom, he unlocked the trunk and peered inside. Reef emerged, stood up, and waved to the cheering brokers. Then, bruised and bloodied, he passed out.

"July 24, 1854. Rec'd $1.00 from R. Atherton for sewing up injuries to head and arm.

Injuries were rec'd inside a trunk rolled over Telegraph Hill. Suggested he use a set of dishes or a crystal chandelier next time."

Record of Surgery
Dr. L. Fenwood

"We were only fifteen."

Reef was not in a mood to explain his bandages, so he had no intention of indulging in any idle chat. He tacked the paper target to the shed at daybreak. He loaded one barrel of the sixteen-inch shot gun, rammed home the load with the rod, and stowed it. Hodges and Sutton approached and took their same positions as Reef faced them and broke the stillness.

"Carl. Glenn."

Carl returned the greeting.

"Good morning, Reef."

"Go ahead, gentlemen, give me a good shaking."

The two messengers began to rock Reef back and forth, side to side. Without much hesitation, Reef turned, shifted his left forearm, pointed the weapon, and fired. The sound of the blast deafened them. Their eyes widened as the paper target was blown away in its entirety, dwarfed by a gaping hole in the shed. The fragmented wood shards followed the shot, blowing an even larger hole out the back.

The men made no move. They remained frozen in their positions. They all sensed that the climax was yet to come. No shed could stand that kind of punishment. As if to confirm their communion, the shed creaked. It groaned, and then it collapsed before them with a thunderous roar. The three men were in awe and remained so for a full minute.

The two messengers turned, and walked away at a half-pace. Reef continued to stare at the ruins in disbelief. What had he created? What power had he unleashed? After a few paces, Hodges stopped, turned, and walked back. He removed his gun belt, with its Pocket Model pistol, and retrieved the shot gun from Reef's hand. He placed the belt and pistol on Reef's shoulder, and walked away with his new weapon. Reef continued to stare at the wreckage in disbelief.

That night, Reef was smiling as he donned his paper hat, feather and breastplate. A piece of the shed was on the table, along with Hodges' pistol and belt. Anita, Mimi, and J.J. were laughing as Reef related the latest event, picked up the pistol, and addressed Anita.

"Here is Carl's pistol. He told me to keep it. My gift to you."

"Thank you, sir. I accept. Will you teach me how to use it?"

"Of course. And, here is a piece of the shed. For your souvenirs."

"Thank you, sir. J.J., what can we do with this?"

J.J. took it, stood it up, and pretended to shoot it down.

"Blam."

They all laughed. As the laughter subsided, Anita and Reef looked at each other. How she loved these precious moments with him. He was so vulnerable, and she loved to embarrass him. Even her family seemed to sense her romantic tension and demanded her to relieve it. This time, though, Anita was embarrassed, and she turned away. J.J. was too young to understand.

"Aren't you going to kiss him, Mommy?"

The revelation of J.J.'s relationship to Anita drew a noticeable reaction from Reef. Anita ignored it, but her embarrassment ripened.

"Bedtime, J.J. Let's go."

She marched him off to bed, closing the door behind her. Reef imposed upon Mimi to clarify what had just happened.

"Anita is J.J.'s mother?"

"Of course. Didn't you know?"

Reef was confused.

"But he calls her 'Annie,' and Al 'Daddy.' "

Mimi was trying to make light of the situation.

"Everyone calls Al 'Daddy,' and J.J. heard us call her 'Annie' long before he ever learned the meaning of the word *Mommy*."

"But where is her husband?"

"She doesn't have one."

Reef was perplexed.

"But surely --"

"The father was a street orphan. We let him stay here for a while. One day, he took off and never returned."

She arose, removed her apron, straightened the chairs, and then started to leave the room.

"It's getting late, and I get up early. Good night, Reef."

"Goodnight, Mimi."

As Mimi left the room, Anita returned. Her eyes engaged Reef's for a saddened exchange, which she cut short. She walked over to the desk, opened a drawer, and removed her diary. She sat down beside Reef on the sofa. Reef spoke first.

"You were playing a joke on me, weren't you?"

Tears began to form in her eyes. She nodded. "Yes."

"How long were you planning to continue it?"

"I'm sorry. I shouldn't have done it."

"How did it happen? Who was he?"

Anita began to cry.

"We were only fifteen. He was an orphan, staying with us. I didn't know what we were doing. It just happened. Then, a few days later, he just left."

"Just like that?"

"Just like that. He left for Angel's Camp, I think. He was always talking about Angel's Camp. I studied reading and writing just so I could write to him but he never answered. I never saw him again. I don't have anything to remember him by. Only this poem I wrote after J.J. was born. Would you like to hear it?"

He didn't want to hear it, but he gave her permission.

"Please."

"It's called, *I Cannot Let You Go.*"

She began to read to him, glancing up to meet his gaze from time to time.

"So young, so bright, so new, like me,
I saw you there one childhood day.
I gave my heart, and when you left,
'Goodbye,' I never got to say."

Reef began to feel nervous. He did not like poetry, but he wanted to be close to the trembling girl. He remained stoic and motionless as she continued.

"You had your destiny to seek,
I know that I had mine. Although
Your trails led you away from me,
I never really let you go."

What was the poem saying anyway? Reef fought the urge to shift to a more comfortable position on the sofa, but that would take him farther away from her, and her nearness was beginning to stir him to action.

"The gold you sought I kept within
My heart, and there I keep it still.
It's there for you, for only you.
To me, return, some day you will."

How long would this go on, anyway? What had she written to the maggot, a novel in verse?

"I searched for you when days had past.
I thought, by chance, at least that we
Could be the best of friends again,
But even that is not to be.

That's all. I never finished it."

She returned the poem to the diary. Small tears descended from her eyes. She was embarrassed at baring her soul. Reef had not liked her poem. She could sense it. Reef was oblivious to her suffering at first. He had not understood her poem, but he understood what he was about to do, what he had wanted to do for so long.

He tilted her chin to face him, and kissed her. At first, she returned his kiss, then broke away, and buried her head in his embrace. She was unable to see the guilt and worry on his face.

He should not be doing this to her. She had confessed, but he had not. Her secret was out. His was not. He was still married to Robin. He should not be kissing Anita. He should not be wanting her, but he did. He did.

After restraining himself for another silent minute, he overcame his guilt, abandoned any thought of confessing, and kissed her again. He would not allow her to cut his kiss short this time and his mounting passion was returned in kind.

Her kiss was apportioned to him somehow in waves of passion, something that he had never experienced with Robin. Just when he thought their kiss was complete, she was there with more to spare. He had kissed her once and had received a half dozen in return.

"August 3, 1854 ... Tonight, he kissed me. He knows about my sin, and he kissed me anyway. I hope he liked it as much as I did."

Diary of Anita Travis

"You bring the money. I bring the girl. We trade"

Lin Thai-Saing saw Boles approaching, nodded to him, then took Caralina by the arm, and led her down a secluded path among the ships. Lin Wu followed them. Thai-Saing whispered to the girl.

"I'm selling you now. You're worth plenty. I sell you to this man. You work for him. Then, you run away from him. Run back to Thai-Saing and I will buy you many pretty dresses and pairs of shoes. You be good now. Look pretty and smile for him."

He motioned to Lin Wu to take the girl, then turned and spoke to Boles in confidence.

"You come to buy my Caralina? Twenty-five hundred dollars. You bring gold? We go inside. The authorities must not see. Not hear."

"No. My friend will buy her, not me. I want to set the time and place. My friend needs time to raise that kind of money. Two months from today. Someplace in the open. Not here."

Thai-Saing thought a moment. He did not like to transact this kind of business in the open.

"Two months from this day. This time. This place. You bring the gold. I'll bring Caralina."

"What about him?"

"He's my friend. You bring your friend and I'll bring mine. I'll bring Caralina. You bring twenty-five hundred dollars in gold coins. We'll trade and everyone will be happy."

Boles agreed. He exchanged glances with Caralina, who turned away from him. Boles turned and walked away. He was glad to be out of there and into the light again. He wanted to meet Atherton at the hotel and relate the meeting plans to him. They could have dinner and a drink together. Dinner and a drink that he felt was well earned and well deserved. Atherton would be a good man to have along on November tenth.

"September 10, 1854 ... The supplier wants $250 in gold for the surgical supplies. Meet me at the Barclay on November 10th. Atherton knows."
        Charlie Boles
        Letter to Ellis Trowbridge

"Shooting. You need more practice shooting."

Reef stood behind Anita, who was facing the collapsed shed. He placed Carl's pistol in her right hand and positioned her left arm to bring her hands together.

"Now, use your thumb. Pull the hammer back all the way, until it stops."

Anita thumbed the hammer to the half-cock position. She was enjoying the moments spent in Reef's arms, especially when he pretended to ignore the pleasure that her nearness was giving him. She turned her head to bring her face closer to his.

"Now, what?"

"Now, nothing. You're only half-cocked."

Anita giggled at Reef's choice of words.

"I'm what?"

"You're only half-cocked. You didn't pull the hammer back all the way. A gun won't go off half-cocked."

Anita was filling with excitement, and continued laughing at Reef's choice of words. She brought the hammer to its full-cock position.

"Oh. I was thinking of something else. Now what?"

"Point it. Aim carefully, and squeeze the trigger."

She aimed and squeezed off a shot. The force of the blast recoiled her arms almost to a vertical position.

"Wow. That's fun."

She laughed and looked back at him for the third time, bringing her mouth closer to his. He did not notice that she had full-cocked the pistol for the next shot. He was too busy figuring out how best to satisfy his appetite for her to be aware of anything else.

"You're fun, too."

He kissed her, pinning her left arm. She responded with a return kiss and a hug with her free right arm, pistol and all. Still oblivious to the danger, he interrupted her half-dozen kisses to proclaim.

"And you're a good student."

He kissed her again, which she returned with all her might, her free arm, and fist. Her index finger contracted and fired the pistol next to Reef's ear with a deafening roar. Reef parted from her in haste.

"My God."

"Oh, Reef. I'm sorry. Did I hurt you?"

"No, I guess not. Not this time, anyway, but you need more practice."

"Oh, yes, Reef. I do. I really do."

She came to him and positioned her mouth to offer another kiss, but he held her back.

"Shooting. You need more practice shooting."

Making a face at him, Anita returned to her lesson, and fired off three more shots in slow succession. She watched with interest as Reef loaded each chamber with powder and a lead ball, compressed the ball with the loading lever, and applied the grease and cap with care.

With equal care, she took her position, cocked, aimed, and fired the five rounds. It was her turn to load the pistol. She loaded it and fired five more rounds, reloaded, and then fired five more. With each round fired, and with full concentration, she was determined to get better. She wanted so much for Reef to be proud of her.

"September 15, 1854 ... He kissed me again today, and I nearly shot him. It frightened him out of his skin, but his face did not turn red! Oh, when can I tell him that I love him? When?"

Diary of Anita Travis

"She only loves the boy she kisses."

Anita finished writing the letter while Mimi and Daddy Al waited in silence. Reef was pacing. The sun was already streaking across the morning sky, and he wanted to get started. Anita was holding him up. She was being stubborn, and reluctant to perform her annual ritual to placate her parents.

"I haven't the slightest idea where he is. How should I address the letter this year?"

"Just address it, *Northern Mines*, the same as last year," responded Mimi. Daddy Al addressed Reef.

"We have her write to J.J.'s father on the boy's birthday. Either he never gets the letter, or he doesn't bother to answer. Can you take the letter with you to the camps?"

Reef was reluctant to get involved. He did not care about finding J.J.'s renegade father. On the other hand, it was a legitimate request of a messenger, and if Anita posted it with his company, he would have to deliver it anyway.

"I'll see what I can do. I'll be in the camps for a few weeks. I'll pass it among our agents. Someone might have heard of him."

Mimi sensed Reef's and Anita's reluctance, and wished to ease their anguish.

"Daddy and I have seen you together. Before things go any further, we want Anita to try just one more time."

Anita was not in a mood to be writing the letter.

"I don't like this. At all."

Reef was beginning to understand the parent's reasoning, and he spoke to the girl.

"Maybe he needs to know that he has a family that loves him."

"I doubt very much that he cares. Besides, it's over. And I don't love him."

"But he's the father of your child. You loved him once."

"We were just children. I'm all grown up, now. And, I don't love him. I lov--"

She looked away from Reef. She had almost revealed her deepest secret, and was seeking a quick alternative.

"I love J.J."

Mimi was quick to intercede.

"Yes, dear, we know you do."

Daddy Al continued to address Reef.

"Thank you for helping us to find him. And have a good trip. We'll see you when you get back."

Daddy Al patted Reef on the back. Mimi embraced Reef, and then accompanied Daddy Al outside. Anita sealed the letter and handed it to Reef, who slipped it into his coat pocket and responded.

"I'll see you in a month."

He kissed her on the cheek and confessed.

"I'm going to miss you."

Anita was disappointed with the perfunctory nature of the kiss. She arose and put her arms around Reef, playful and stand-offish.

"A poem I know says a boy can love *any* girl he misses."

Reef did not get her drift, but played along.

"Oh? And whom does it say a girl can love?"

"She only loves the boy she *kisses*."

She kissed him on the mouth. He returned the kiss for a moment, but mindful of the nature of his postal mission, and her parents outside, he broke away.

"Take care of yourself and don't worry. I'll find him for you. Somehow."

He walked out the door, looked back, and waved. Anita was left alone at the door and spoke to the silence.

"You foolish man. I don't want him somehow. I want you. Somehow."

A tear trickled down her cheek as she watched him disappear down the street.

"October 19, 1854 ... Letter posted to Nathan Burgess, Northern Mines."
Record of Collections
Wells, Fargo & Co. Express

"I'll see you in hell, Atherton ... You'll pay."

        Carson helped Reef load signs, counter cages,
stationery cases, chairs, and other supplies until the
day wagon was piled high. Reef would backtrack on
his return trip and bring back the gold dust from
each office, so he stowed one of the new cut-off shot
guns, and some powder, shot, and wads that the
gunsmith had delivered.
        The men shook hands. Reef climbed into the
wagon, and released the brake. Carson watched the
wagon depart, then returned to the office.
        To reach his destinations in the Northern
Mines, Reef took the ferry to Oakland and the
steamer to Sacramento. Then, he headed east to
reach the primitive trail out of Auburn to Grass
Valley. The agent at Grass Valley helped Reef unload
some supplies and hang a wood office sign. Mindful
of his unpleasant duty, Reef reached into his coat for
Anita's letter and showed it to the agent, who thought
for a moment, and then shook his head. They shook

hands. Reef returned to the wagon and made his way past the tents and on down the trail to the next camp.

The horse and wagon paths took Reef to Nevada City and Rough And Ready. After a dozen days, the wagon was still half full and the quest for J.J.'s father had gone nowhere. The response was always the same. Company agents would think a moment, then shake their heads.

A group of miners would approach the wagon, and Reef would stop and show them Anita's letter. They would look at each other, look back at Reef, and shake their heads. Reef would nod, thank them, then drive on. More camps, offloads, and days spent searching.

At Timbuctoo, it was different. The wagon was almost empty. The agent greeted Reef, and helped him unload the few remaining items. Each man carried two armloads into the office. They unloaded the supplies onto the counter and went behind it, separating themselves from the miners that were reading from a bulletin board, counting money, and filling out exchange forms. Reef was glad that his wagon was empty, signaling that his return to the city would be imminent.

"That's about everything for this trip."

"Where do you go from here?"

"To Marysville. I'll pick up their gold, then come back here to pick up yours the day after tomorrow. Then, back to San Francisco."

"Do you want to stay the night? I have an extra bed in the storeroom."

"No, I'd like to make it to Marysville by nightfall. I'd like a nice hot bath. And a soft, clean bed."

"I don't blame you. Well, have a good trip, Atherton.

"Thanks. Oh, by the way. Have you heard of a miner by the name of Nathan Burgess?"

He handed the agent the letter.

"Yeah. He's just a kid. Sleeps out in back of the Mule Kick Saloon. First four-pole tent on the left past the creek."

He returned the letter. Reef looked at the envelope and questioned the agent.

"What do you know about him?"

"Somewhat of a loner and a drunkard. He has a special account here, but it's usually empty. Drinks or gambles his dust away. Do you want me to deliver it to him?"

"No, I think I'll deliver it myself, if you don't mind."

"Not at all. Save me the trouble. That'll be a dollar for the company, though."

Reef reached into his pocket for a dollar, paid the agent, and left the office. Reef found the saloon, passed it, and walked up to the shelter. Reef saw that Burgess was sleeping and his clothes were ragged. Reef called to him and Burgess woke up groggy and drunk.

"Nathan Burgess?"

"Yeah? Whaddaya want?"

"I have a letter for you. From a Miss Anita Travis."

"I don't have a dollar."

"It's prepaid."

Burgess was unsure in his movements, positioned himself on his hands and knees, and found that he was able to stand up.

By who? Who paid you to bring me a letter?"

"I did."

"You did? Why?"

"Let's just say the letter contains some information that you should have."

Burgess steadied himself, opened the letter, and stared at it. Silence. Burgess was still. He handed the letter to Reef.

"I can't read."

"Do you want me to read it to you?"

"Yeah. Read it to me."

Reef opened the envelope and began reading the letter.

"Dear Nathan. On October 19th, in '49, I gave birth to our son, John Jacob. I know I should be your wife so you can provide for us, but I have no such desire or feelings. My feelings are for --"

Reef reacted to seeing his name in the letter.

"-- a Mr. Atherton, our boarder. Please understand and leave us alone. Sincerely, Anita."

Burgess was angry.

"You Atherton?"

"Yes."

"She had my baby, but she loves you?"

Reef put his hands on Burgess' shoulders to steady him, and to attempt to bring calm to the situation.

"There's no need to be angry. You can come back and do right by them. I won't stand in your way."

Burgess brushed Reef off, getting angrier.

"She's a young one, isn't she, Atherton? What's the matter? Getting old? Can't find someone your own age? Robbing the cradle while her folks are workin'?"

"That's not true. You're out of line."

"Well, you can't take away my girl. I'm keeping her, Atherton. She's mine, so stay out of her bed."

Reef had had enough. He took the miner's shirt in both hands and pulled him to his face.

"You little piss ant. I've thrown bigger and better men than you to the sharks."

And he had. His own words stunned him and flooded him with memories of quelling the mutinies and uprisings on the decks of the *Polar Star*. Memories that he had wanted to forget. But he could not. He could not erase those memories. Men like this, boys like this, always reminded him of what he had been. What he was. He hated Burgess for reminding him. He hated him, but he let him go.

Burgess threw a punch at Reef. Reef fended it off with little effort. Reef turned Burgess around and wrestled him to the ground. Burgess was belligerent, filled with self-pity, and reversed himself.

"Go back. Do right by them. What for? Nuthin' I do works out. You can see that. She loves you. You can have her."

Reef was disgusted with Burgess. The boy had no pride, and no resolve to carry out his duty to take care of his family.

"I'll be happy to give her your message, Burgess."

Burgess reversed himself again.

"I'll see you in hell, Atherton. You can't take my girl and get away without payin'. You hear me? You'll pay. You'll pay."

Burgess closed his eyes, belched, and passed out. Reef released him, got up, and drove his wagon out of the camp.

"November 1, 1854 ... Rec'd $1 from Messenger Atherton, collection for letter delivered to N. Burgess."

Record of Collections
Timbuctoo, Cala.
Wells, Fargo & Co.

"*W*here *we're going, we're all Italian.*"

Trowbridge carried a small bundle. He quick-stepped his way from the lighted passenger dock down a dark passageway. He saw Boles waiting for him.

"Where is she?"

"She's with Thai-Saing. He's ready to meet us."

"Is it far from this alley? I don't want anyone prying, but I want some measure of safety. Where's Atherton?"

"I saw him a few minutes ago. He's around here somewhere. Don't worry. The Chinaman will scare away the curious, and I'm here to back you."

"Very well. I have a firearm. Do you?"

"Yes, Ellis. I do."

"Good. I hope you won't have to use it."

"Neither do I. I've never fired a pistol before."

Trowbridge was startled by Boles' revelation. He hesitated before responding.

"Well. May God be with us, Charlie, why didn't you tell me before?"

"I didn't think it was important. Until now, that is."

"So be it. May God help us. If the occasion arises, though, brandish it lively, Charlie, brandish it lively."

"I will, Ellis. I will."

They walked down a second dark passageway. Lin Thai-Saing, Caralina, and Lin Wu were waiting for them. A floor guard carried a small lantern to give light to the proceedings. Thai-Saing was the first to speak.

"Good evening, gentlemen. Here is my little Caralina. Just like I promised."

Trowbridge replied without taking his eyes off the girl.

"Here is your bond money and expenses. Twenty-five hundred dollars in gold. Do you have the papers?"

Thai-Saing smiled, shrugged his shoulders, and began to count the money. When he was finished counting, he smiled and opened his hands, palms upward, toying with Trowbridge. Wu stepped forward from behind. Trowbridge became apprehensive. What was Thai-Saing doing, and why was Wu so close? Wu dropped a paper in Thai-Saing's open palm and stepped back. Trowbridge was relieved. Thai-Saing handed over the bond.

"Ah, here is the bond. You now own sweet little Caralina."

Thai-Saing spoke to the girl.

"Goodbye, little song bird. You belong to this man now. He has promised to take good care of you."

Trowbridge examined the bond in the light, nodded, and placed it inside his coat. He took her by the hand, led her away with Boles, and stopped when he reached better light. He unwrapped the bundle to reveal a new cloak and hood of rich green silk and velvet with gold embroidery. He stooped and wrapped it around Caralina with care. He picked her up in his arms and carried her. Caralina was pleased with the gift, but uncertain and troubled about her future.

She was scared and she began to cry. Her grey homespun dress was wrinkled and dirty, and her mismatched long-stockings sagged from her calves and slipped down over the tops of her old black shoes with the missing buttons. She wore the only clothes that remained after the girls had found out that she would be leaving.

Her only friends had taken all of her pretty dresses, her shoes with the gold buckles and her stockings, her silk underwear, slips, and chemisettes, her combs and brushes, her rouges, and her bows and ribbons. Everything. Everything that made her pretty.

They took them, they fought over them, and then, they avoided her. They pretended not to know her. As though she was never there. Only "Shu Shu" came to hug her and kiss her and say goodbye. The thought of Shu-Chuan brought Caralina back to the present and reminded her of her duty to be polite and to please her new owner.

"Do you want me to sing and dance for you, Mister?"

Trowbridge kissed her on the cheek, and caressed her.

"No, my little one. You won't have to sing and dance any more. Come now. I want you to meet someone."

"Who?"

"You'll see."

Trowbridge took her toward a bench, out in the light and activity of the street. Madelaine was sitting there, waiting.

"See the lady sitting there on the bench?"

"Who is she?"

"She is a very nice lady. She would like very much to be your stepmother."

When Trowbridge reached the bench with the girl, he addressed his wife.

"My dear, I have a gift for you. A little girl."

Trowbridge placed Caralina on the bench, then returned to join Boles a few paces away. Beth Ellen came up to Trowbridge and took his arm. Tears were glistening in her eyes. He took her hand, caressed it, and held it for comfort.

"Yes, my darling, I know. It's your turn. And, you want a boy."

Madelaine embraced Caralina, and then whispered to her.

"Hello, my little girl."

Caralina looked at Madelaine's face, her clothes, and her hat. Then she looked at herself, then again at Madelaine. Madelaine embraced her again, and pressed the girl's head to her shoulder.

"What is your name?"

"My name is Caralina."

"Yes. I know. What is your family name?"

"Vestoni. It's Italian."

"Yes, that would be Italian, wouldn't it?"

"Mama told me once, if ever I felt a tear trickle from my eye, if ever I was hurting so much that I could not even cry, if ever I felt so alone that even God did not want me, then I would know what it meant to be Italian. Are you Italian?"

"Oh, sweet girl, yes. If that's what it takes to be Italian, I suppose that I am. I suppose where we're going, we're all Italian."

"You're so soft. You smell so good. And I feel so dirty. Are you sure that you really want me?"

Madelaine kissed and hugged her, repeating the girls own affirmation.

"Well, I'm here, aren't I?"

Thai-Saing was tiring of the tender scene. Thai-Saing motioned for Wu and the guard to follow the Mormons.

"Follow these religious fanatics. Find out where they take her. The judge will issue a fugitive slave warrant and put these fools in jail. He will return Caralina to me and I will have their gold besides."

Wu and the guard departed. Thai-Saing grinned then broke into laughter, which drowned the noise of the pistol's hammer being pulled to its full-cock position. Reef stepped from behind piles of abandoned crates and shoved the pistol into Thai-Saing's throat.

"I'll take my money back, now."

Thai-Saing froze. He had made the mistake of separating himself from his guards. Reef reached inside Thai-Saing's coat and retrieved the gold paid by Trowbridge.

"The next time you jump a claim, make sure the job gets finished. Walk to the street."

Reef turned the Chinaman and pushed him toward the busy street. When they reached the main stream of traffic, noise, and activity, Reef stowed his pistol and disappeared from Thai-Saing's sight and from the glare of hatred that followed with it.

> *"November 10, 1854 ... Rec'd $2500 gold specie, gen'l deposit for Dr. Ellis Trowbridge."*
>   *Twelve*
>   *Record of Money Receipts*
>   *Wells, Fargo & Co.*

"Reef is my husband, not my owner."

In December of 1854, Paul Duchard was not thinking of Christmas. Amid shouting in the streets and angry depositors banging on the bank doors, he was sitting behind his desk as the clerk knocked and entered.

"The newspaper, sir. Panic is rampant in the streets outside."

"Yes, I hear."

The clerk placed the newspaper on the desk. The bold lines at the heads of two columns told the story.

> *PAGE, BACON & CO. DEFAULTS.*
> *ADAMS & CO. CLOSES DOORS.*

"Will that be all, sir?"

"Yes, thank you."

Robin entered as the clerk left and closed the door. Duchard rose. She crossed the room and greeted him with a warm embrace.

"You know, Paul?"

"Yes, I know. We can't meet our demands. I'm ruined."

Duchard sat and threw the newspaper into the wire basket. Robin attempted to comfort him.

"Speak with father, Paul. He'll take you into the firm."

"Your father? How can I face him? He was shrewd. He bought our good investments. I bought Page Bacon's. Mine are worthless."

"Oh, Paul. You can't just give up. The world doesn't end here."

"Doesn't it? I have nothing left, Robin. I'll have to declare insolvency."

"You'll work your way out of it. Look at Reef. He survived."

"Reef. My only competitor and he doesn't even know it. The irony of it all. I'll follow him to California and strike it rich."

"He's not rich. He quit the gold mining venture. He works in San Francisco, now."

"Doing what?"

"God knows. I'm not sure. Shipping, I think. Merchandising. I don't know. I don't even want to know. Whatever it is, it isn't bringing in much money."

"When is he coming back?"

"He won't say. He's too ashamed. He's a failure again."

"Why don't you forget him, Robin?"

"What do you mean? He's my husband."

"Get a dissolution. So we can be married. We love each other, and we belong together, Robin."

Robin was annoyed.

"Just like that? After what's happened? You're just as penniless as he is. Dissolve one marriage in favor of leaping into another? That doesn't sound like me.

"But why not? It's not like we're being impulsive or leaping into anything. We love each other. Why not?"

"You know perfectly well, why not. Eventually, you would gain control of father's fortune and you would lose that, too. I will stay with Reef. At least, he doesn't want father's money."

"You still love him, don't you, Robin?"

"Don't be silly. Reef is my husband, not my owner. I am my father's heiress, and I don't intend to give that up. Not to Reef and not to you. You're on your own, Paul. Will you speak with father, or not?"

Duchard had no further proposals to make.

"Yes, Robin, I will speak to your father. Is that what you want? To keep me around? Close at hand? For your convenience? Like tonight, perhaps?"

"No. Not tonight. Not ever. You work it out with father, but do not include me in your plans. Good day, Paul."

Paul moved to embrace her. She avoided his embrace and departed. Duchard sat at his desk. He had lost everything.

"December 12, 1854 ... Paul Duchard, banker, formerly with Adams & Company, has joined the prestigious firm of Larimore & Company."

The Boston News-Letter

"Adams has stopped paying on demands."

News of the bank failures reached San Francisco in ten weeks. When the ship first telegraphed its doomsday message to the brokers on Telegraph Hill, they deserted their posts to a man and fled to their respective banks to withdraw their general accounts.

Adams & Company, Rhodes & Lusk Express Company, Wells, Fargo & Company, and Page, Bacon & Company were besieged with depositors running from Telegraph Hill, then from the nearby shops, then from the docks, and eventually from every direction in the city.

Crazed miners, merchants, and sailors were united in their quest of presenting their demands and withdrawing their wealth to safer environments than Montgomery Street.

Carson was grabbing depositors and slowing them by force in their rush to get into the Wells Fargo office.

"Now calm down. Your deposits are safe. Just line up and you'll be paid."

One or two depositors might take heart, but the majority persisted in their efforts to beat their competitors to the line that was forming inside the office. Soon, the line was out the door and into the street, blocking all traffic that was not afoot. Depositors responded with whatever emotion spoke best their fears.

"I'll feel a lot better when it's in my pocket instead of yours."

Carson was not to be intimidated by angry customers.

"Line up, and you'll be paid. Rush this door, and you'll go to the end of the line."

Reef and J.J. were coming up the street. Reef noticed the commotion, then took J.J. by the hand as a precaution. Carson saw them approaching, motioned for Reef to hurry, then escorted him and J.J. inside the bank. They entered Carson's office and Reef closed the door behind them.

"What's happened?"

"The *California* just docked. Banks in the East are failing to meet their demands. Page Bacon has closed its doors, and Adams may be right behind them."

"How do we stand?"

"Most of our dust is shipped to the mint right away, so we're fine in town. The camps may have problems though, if we can't get gold to them fast enough."

J.J. left the office and walked toward the stable. Reef continued.

"What can I do?"

"Ten and eleven are already on their way to some of the camps with all the coins we can spare. I need you to present some demands on Adams."

Carson walked to the safe and opened it. He picked up a bundle of exchange drafts and handed them to Reef. His voice carried an accent of worry, but it was filled with determination.

"Adams has stopped paying on drafts here in town. When the miners in the camps find out, they'll riot and burn Adams' offices. The news hasn't reached the camps, yet. Get there first. Go to as many Adams offices as you can and cash these demands."

"I'll need money for fresh horses. And get word to the Travises. See that J.J. gets home, what with that mob in the streets."

Carson removed some coins and a letter from the safe and closed it.

"I will. I'll tell them you'll be gone about a week. Here's one hundred dollars and a company letter of credit. I'll saddle Cap for you and tie Kirk in tow. They're both sixteen hands, strong, and fast. When both are done in, leave them at a livery and hire more."

They arose and left the office. Carson continued his directives.

"As you collect on the demands, stop at our offices. Give each agent enough gold to cover the general accounts. Don't concern yourself with special accounts. They're covered. Be sure and get a receipt from each agent."

Carson escorted Reef into the stable and saddled one of the horses while Reef gathered up a bedroll, water flask, and a week's provisions. Twenty minutes later, Reef was ready. He bid Carson goodbye, mounted Cap, took Kirk in tow, and rode out the door past the noisy depositors.

> *"Feb'y 23, 1855 ... $100 gold paid to Atherton for expenses, S.F. to Northern mines."*
>
> *Expense Ledger*
> *Wells, Fargo & Co.*

"For six months, I will teach her everything ..."

Nathan Burgess was glad to get off the steamer and return his feet to solid ground. He stepped aside to let other passengers rush ahead. He was nursing his hangover, and was in no hurry. He took a swig from a bottle and returned it to his pack.

Lin Thai-Saing and his girls were at work, but business was not that good. Two passengers were annoyed at being delayed by one girl. They ignored her proposition, rejected her song and dance, and shoved her aside. Another girl spotted the slow-moving Burgess and moved to confront him. Thai-Saing stood aside and watched.

"Sing a song for the handsome miner? I'll take you to heaven for five pinches."

Burgess was dirty, unshaven, and reeked of vomit, but was by no means too self-conscious to pass up a pretty girl's petition. He offered her his gold poke.

"Sure, pretty girl. I haven't been with a girl as pretty as you for a long time. Anita Travis was her name. What's yours?"

Thai-Saing focused his attention on the miner who had spoken Anita's name. The girl took the gold poke, handed it to Thai-Saing, and began her song and dance. Burgess reached for his gold poke.

"Hey, let her pinch. Not you."

"You want her? I take five pinches. You don't want her? I'll take two for telling you how you can make lots of money."

Burgess moved to grab his poke.

"Give it back."

Thai-Saing pulled the poke back, out of Burgess' reach. Lin Wu moved toward Burgess to intervene, but was restrained by Thai-Saing. Thai-Saing pursued his intention to gain the confidence of the miner.

"Mister. Please. Lin Thai-Saing means you no harm, but I must look after my little girl. She has need of food and pretty things. Her fingers are so thin and mine are so fat. You will forgive my business methods, will you not? Come. Let us talk business. You can make much money with Lin Thai-Saing."

Thai-Saing returned the gold poke to Burgess undebited. Burgess was pleased to get his poke back, but was suspicious. Nobody ever did him any favors. What was different now?

"Money? Me make money? How?"

"Come. Let us walk to my chambers. Ahead, in the ship, *Polar Star*. A gallant ship, indeed. It brought many miners to this shore, just like you, but it was abandoned. Just like you. Lin Thai-Saing sees the value in *Polar Star*. Lin Thai-Saing sees value in you, Mister. Come."

Thai-Saing led the group in the direction of his brothel. When they arrived, Thai-Saing let Burgess enter, and then motioned to the others to continue their solicitations. He escorted the young miner to his quarters, indicated a seat for Burgess, and took one for himself.

Two attractive young sing-song girls brought pillows and drinks for the two men. The girls removed the miner's boots, then placed one of the pillows under his feet and the other behind his head. One girl began to massage his neck and shoulders while the other served his drink. Thai-Saing continued his pitch.

"My name is Lin Thai-Saing. Tell me your name, and tell me about your sweetheart."

"Burgess. Nathan Burgess. My girl is Anita Travis. She had my baby. A boy."

Lin Thai-Saing was successful at restraining his glee. His eyes widened.

"Is that so? A son. How proud you must be. To have a wife to work for you. And, to have a son. These are two of life's greatest treasures."

"She's not my wife, and she doesn't work for me. I haven't seen her in five years."

"Haven't seen her? How is that?"

"I've been in the mines. I want out of there. Yeah, I want her to work for me."

"Maybe sing songs and give pleasure to you and your friends for money, like my girls do for me?"

"Yeah."

"But I can teach your Anita. Like I taught my girls. I will teach Anita to work for you. Then you can be a respected businessman, too. Like Lin Thai-Saing."

"You can do that?"

"Of course. You are a bright young man. She should work for you and bring you the respect of a businessman, like me."

Burgess was suspicious.

"What do you want in return?"

"A small token of service. A bond. If you marry her, you can bond her to work for me. For six months, I will teach her everything that she needs to know. I will take my fees and expenses from her earnings and pass the balance on to you. Thereafter, she will work for you alone."

"You can do that?"

"Of course. And you will want to bond your son to me, as well. You will be busy, traveling, meeting people, and doing business, like Lin Thai-Saing. Not good for you to be tied down to a child. I can teach the boy, and he will work for you, too."

"And I don't have to do anything?"

"Of course. You must work hard. To invest the money that your wife and son will earn for you. After all, life is not without balance."

"Collect the money and invest it."

"Collect the money. Invest it. Become respected. Like Lin Thai-Saing."

"Bonding is against the law. How can we get away with that?"

"A gentlemen's agreement. I will speak with Anita. She will soon see that to work for Lin Thai-Saing and for you is the best thing for the boy."

"Yeah. What's best for my son."

"Of course. Now. Stay here tonight. These pretty girls will bring you food and more to drink. They will sing their songs, dance with you, and give you pleasure all night long. You will be my honored guest."

Lin Thai-Saing motioned to the girls. They caressed and touched Burgess, then took him by the hands. He arose and followed them to a large crib. Lin Thai-Saing nodded his approval and smiled.

"March 1, 1855 ... $ 1.00 Passage Paid."
Passenger's Receipt
Oakland-San Francisco Ferry

"... You grant my wish and we become one."

The Barclay Hotel welcomed a constant stream of guests that fed a resonating hum of activity. Desk clerks, maids, and servants concentrated on checking people into rooms, checking them out, giving directions, dispensing towels, cooking meals, mixing drinks, and lighting cigars.

A large stack of *Alta Californias* announced that "Adams & Co. Is Insolvent," and greeted each guest at the main desk. The lobby was filled with smoke, aromas from the dining room, and the heated *cussions and discussions* of the relative merits and demerits of the American banking system.

Reef was already aware of the news. He had experienced it first-hand, and was not inclined to waste any time reading or talking about it. He was eager to get back to the office, and he waved off the paper offered by the clerk.

"I'm Atherton. Wells Fargo. Do you have business with me?"

"Frankly, no. I already withdrew my money. However, our guest in two-oh-four might have a different answer for you."

"Your guest? Who is he and what does he want with me?"

"Mister, I don't ask my guests those kinds of questions."

The clerk peered at the register and enjoyed his game of fingering the pages, looking for the name of the occupant in Room 204.

"However, *her* name is --"

"Robin Atherton," interrupted Robin.

Reef turned, stunned to hear the sound of her voice.

"Robin."

She came closer to him.

"Yes. Robin. Your lost love. Do you remember me?"

She greeted him with a warm embrace and brush-kissed him on the mouth, ever aware of prying eyes of the clerk, hotel domestics, curious guests, and miscellaneous riff-raff. The topic of discussion in the lobby had taken a mid-course correction.

Reef said nothing. He moved from shock, to surprise, to delight. Then, he reversed his spectrum of emotions. He put his arms around her and held her fast, oblivious to the growing merriment surrounding them. Robin was quite aware of the spectacle and moved to gain her release. She whispered to him.

"Let's go to the room, dear. Our feelings demand some privacy."

Reef was still shocked to see her, but more than pleased to be led by her soft, warm hand up the stairs, down the hall, and into her room. The onlookers were disappointed to see them disappear, and speculated with high spirits upon what circumstances had parted the lovers, and with jovial merriment upon what was about to take place at their delicious reunion.

Reef shut the door behind him, still speechless. Robin put her arms around him, and gave him a long best-ever kiss.

"Reef. I missed you so much."

She kissed him again, and he returned the kiss with a flood of passion and platitudes.

"It's been so long. Not one day passed."

Robin interrupted him with another kiss.

"I know. I know."

Then she gave him another. And another. She was intent upon re-establishing her claim to her husband and he was responding according to plan.

"Robin. My little bird. My precious little bird."

Robin placed her hand on his mouth. Her voice intoned a sense of urgency and fear.

"Reef. Tell me what happened."

That was her special plea, words that Reef had not heard in almost two years. They signaled the beginning of *Revelations*, the passion game that she had started on their wedding night ten years ago.

Their mutual recitals heighten their pleasure when each lover in turn reveals the most private and personal thoughts and intentions, and describes aloud the most intimate details of their lovemaking.

"What happened?" asked Robin, beckoning him to play the game with her.

Reef tugged on her waist to close the distance between them. He ran his hands up her back and into her hair.

"Reef. Tell me what happened," she intoned.

"I moved my hands up her tiny back and into her cascading hair."

"Why did you do that, Reef?"

"I was aching to have her. Her scent was so fresh."

"What happened then, Reef?"

Reef pressed his face into her hair and began kissing her as he continued to describe the activity.

"I buried my face in her hair, and kissed her cheeks, and her beautiful mouth. Tell me what happened then, Robin."

It was her turn. She described his actions and her perceptions of them.

"His hands moved from my hair, down my back, and he began unbuttoning my dress. He kissed me again. So wet. So intense. He took off his coat, and began unbuttoning his shirt. And then what happened, Reef?"

God, his clothes look ragged. Oh, my God, what a horrible scar. What happened to him? He's so thin. Don't be distracted. Put it out of your mind. Let him speak. Listen. And play.

"Tell me, Reef."

"We undressed each other. We let the clothes drop to the floor. I picked her up, and held her. So light in my arms. So beautiful. I took her to the bed, placed her on it, and prepared her. Tell me, Robin."

"He was so gentle. This big sea animal. The way he looked at my body thrilled me. He touched me and kissed me again. I wanted him so. I didn't want to wait any longer. Tell me, Reef, tell me."

"I brought our bodies together. I felt her tight embrace. Her nails. We kissed. We kissed again. I began to take my relief with her. Describe it, Robin. What is it like?"

"I want his intrusion. And he indulges me. Again. Again. You grant my wish. We are one. And I will never. Let go. Of you. Aga-in. Aga-in. A-ga-i-n."

Robin struggled under the weight and panted for air. Her own loud gratification was lost in the boisterous and unbridled exaltations of her spent husband. God, he is good. Just as good as ever.

Except for his hand. He only used one hand to play this time. She would have to ask him about that later and about his clothes. He looked dreadful. She would buy him some new clothes, but now it was time for sleep. God, he is good. So good.

Reef awakened when Robin turned to face him and put her head upon his chest. She guided her flowing perfumed hair from beyond her pillow down around his head and over part of his face. Reef knew that holding him in this manner was her favorite morning wake-up position. With such proximity to all of her feminine gifts, he was never able to resist her subsequent requests, physical or otherwise. He wondered what she would ask of him this time. He looked around the room, now darkened by the receding sunlight, and remembered his intention to return to the bank. Robin sensed that he was beginning to stir, so she pretended to awaken.

"Reef, don't get up. Stay in bed with me."

"I have to get to the bank. Just for a few hours. Then I'll be back."

Reef was enthusiastic. She was not. She placed her cheek on his chest and moved her gaze back and forth over their bodies. She looked at his weak hand. The lack of movement concerned her but she would inquire about it later.

"Why do you have to go? Don't they close the bank at sundown?"

"No, this is not Boston. We take a gold shipment to the docks whenever a ship leaves for Panama."

"Hold me. Just for a few minutes. Tell me about your work. What do you do there?"

"I buy all manner of things for our company. Supplies. Equipment. Things that we need to transact our business. Then, I deliver them to our agents in the gold camps."

Robin winced.

"Deliver?"

"Yes. You'll have to see it. Hundreds of miners in the streams, digging for gold. Come with me on my next trip, Robin."

She shuddered.

"Go with you? To the camps?"

"Yes. They're almost shoulder to shoulder. In the streams, panning the gold."

Robin was apprehensive. What was 'panning?'

"Panning?"

"Yes. They dig gold right out of the streams. Wagonloads of it. We have twenty-six offices now. Miners bring their gold to us. We bring it to San Francisco and ship it to New York. I've lost the *Polar Star*, but I can buy others like her and ship gold on my ships, Robin. Our ships. We'll become wealthy. We could be happy here."

Robin rolled her eyes upward.

"But where would we live? In one of those camps?"

Reef laughed.

"Oh, no. We'd live right here in San Francisco."

Robin gagged to herself. He answered each of her questions with a smile, caressing her body, or lifting her chin and kissing her on the forehead, cheek, or mouth. She was becoming annoyed and decided to change the subject, while Reef responded with increasing excitement.

"Reef. Where do you live now?"

"Daddy Al's boarding house. Up Market Street about a mile and a half from here."

"Daddy Al's. Boarding house."

Robin's face reflected a look of dread.

"Reef. Could we stay here at the hotel for now?"

"Yes, we can stay here, but I'll have to get my clothes. Right now, I have to get back to the bank."

"Reef."

"Yes?"

"In the morning. When you go to the bank, may I go to Daddy Al's? I want to feel useful, Reef. I can arrange to have your things brought here. I came to take care of you, dear. To help you out. Especially since you're so busy."

Perfect. She could break the news to Anita.

"Yes, do that. Tell the Travises that I'll come by later. Some of the company's things are there, and I need to pick them up."

"I will, dear."

Robin's kiss was warm and moist, a kiss that he returned with equal fervor, one that she refused to break off, and one that delayed his return to the office by an additional five minutes. Fifteen minutes. Thirty minutes.

> " *March 8, 1855 ... Although his hand was weakened by a shot wound, his manly presence in my chamber is more potent and kinetic than I can ever recall.*"
> *Robin Larimore Atherton*
> *Letter to Sarah Carswell*

"Anita. Dear Anita, I married him."

Robin sat on the sofa and contemplated the depressing surroundings. Why would anyone live in such a wretched dwelling, much less a refined Bostonian like Reef? What could have been the attraction? Her question was answered as soon as it was posed. Anita walked in the door and was surprised to see a strange woman in the house.

"Oh. Hello."

"Hello. The neighbor suggested that I enter and wait. Is that all right?"

"Yes, it is. People do that all the time. What do you want?"

"Mr. Atherton told me that this is where he lives. Is that true?"

"Yes, he lives here. I'm Anita."

Her face announced her surprise and recognition. She joined Robin on the sofa.

"Oh. I know you. You're the lady in the dogtype."

"Dogtype? I beg your pardon?"

"Yes, the photograph that Reef carries with him."

"Reef? Oh, the daguerr-, yes, the dogtype."

She ignored the disgusting slang and continued.

"He carries my photograph with him?"

"Yes, always. Except when he puts it on the dresser."

"I see. And I understand why he lives here. You're very friendly."

"So are you. You're beautiful. Are you here to take him away from me?"

"He doesn't really belong here, does he? He really belongs back in Boston, with me."

"Seems to me, he should be where he wants, and with who he wants."

Robin laughed. Was this little pauper serious? What was her name? Anita?

"Meaning here, Anita? With you?"

Anita sensed that she was the object of Robin's sport, and her anger registered in her face.

"I love him. I can be his girl, too, you know. You don't own him."

The little hussy. She didn't know. Reef had not told her. The louse. Robin was enjoying this more than ever.

"Oh, is that so? Anita, dear, I'm more than just his girl. Didn't he tell you?"

"What do you mean?"

Robin relished the moment. She put on her best sad face, and let the words flow out like bittersweet honey.

"Anita. Dear Anita, I married him."

The words stunned Anita. Her face filled with shock and disbelief, and tears began to well in her eyes. Robin continued to cut into the girl.

"He didn't tell you, did he? The Casanova. But then, I'm not surprised. That is so like him."

Anita began sobbing, and it was apparent that she could not stop. Robin moved to comfort her, handing her a handkerchief, and marveling at the intensity of the girl's grief. Here was a problem. Robin would have to find a way to sever the girl's attachment to Reef. She embraced the girl and stroked her hair.

"Now, don't cry. You'll get over him. You are young. And *somewhat* attractive. In a pilgrim sort of way. You'll find someone else. More suitable for you. A miner, perhaps. Or a sailor."

She continued to provide comfort, while stifling a smug look and a feeling of satisfaction. Anita cried without restraint for minutes. When she stopped, Robin gave her one long tight squeeze and released her. Anita blew her nose and began to regain her composure. Robin continued her patronage.

"There, there. That's better. See? You feel better already."

Robin waited a moment before plunging the knife in one more time.

"Anita. Dear, when you feel better, would you be good enough to pack his things? And send them to the Barclay Hotel. In care of Mrs. Atherton."

Anita began to cry again.

"Yes'm."

"Thank you, dear."

Robin arose and walked to the door, leaving Anita on the couch. Anita buried her face in her hands and sobbed. Robin turned for a final observation. She noted the proximity of the bedroom doors to each other, and wondered how often Reef and the girl must have traversed the distance when the parents were not around. She frowned in anticipation of the additional effort that she would have to expend to neutralize the girl's relationship with her handsome banker-to-be.

"March 9, 1855 ... She called me dear. She is married to him. How deep it cut me. I just want to die. I just want the pain to end."

Diary of Anita Travis

"We must see justice done for Mr. Burgess."

Eggs, milk, and sugar. The porch was just as good a place as any to mix eggs, milk, and sugar. Anita sat there alone, preparing her custards for that evening, while Mimi prepared pies in the kitchen. Even though Anita had played the fool and felt smaller than worthless, she still had customers to feed. She was forcing herself to concentrate on eggs, milk and sugar. So much so, that the man approaching the house went almost unnoticed.

This man had a familiar look about him, and she felt waves of fear and dread possess her.

"Oh no. Don't let it be him. Please. Oh, God, it *is* him. He's come back."

Burgess was not drunk, but he swaggered as he walked, and he laughed at the sight of Anita and her custard bowls.

"Hello, 'Custard Annie.' Guess who's back in town?"

"Hello, Nathan."

"I got your letter. Your precious Atherton paid a dollar to have it delivered to me. Then, he delivered it in person. What a fool. We'll have to thank him for bringing our little family together again."

"You're drunk, Nathan. Why did you come back? Why didn't you just stay where you were?"

"Where I was? Workin' in the mines? Why sweet Anita, you'd drink, too, if you had to work the mines. And nuthin' to show for it."

"What do you want?"

"Atherton doesn't want you. He says I can have you. He won't stand in our way. That's what he said. You ask him. He says you and the boy belong to me. So, you can come and work for me, now."

"Doing what?"

"Singing songs. Down at the docks. You can quit selling your stupid pies and custards. Hell, we'll get five pinches for each miner you lay. You're a lively one. Real lively. I remember. Lin Thai-Saing will teach you everything you need to know."

"I won't do it. I won't be a sing-song girl. Not when J.J. was inside me. Not after. And not now. Never. Not for you. Not for anyone. You get outta here, and leave us alone."

Mimi heard Anita shouting and came to the doorway.

"You heard her, Nathan. Get out of here, and don't come back. We take care of her and J.J. just fine without you. She isn't gonna sleep with you or any of your trashy friends. Now go."

"We'll see about that, you high and mighty nose-in-the-air. She'll be a proper wife to me, plain and simple. Do what I say, when I say, and where I say. You'll see. The judge'll see it my way. Just wait."

Burgess turned and walked away, somewhat sobered by the effort expended in the argument. Mimi looked at Anita with a face yet filled with anger. Anita started to cry, but held back her tears and stood up.

"You stay away from me and my baby, Nathan."

"I'll go and make up the bed, sweet Anita. You get yourself ready for a weddin'. You'll sing plenty for me and my friends on your weddin' night. At five pinches each," Burgess taunted her.

"You stay away," sobbed Anita.

She turned and went inside to retrieve her Bible. She removed the poem and tore it into pieces on the way out the door, flinging it at the departing miner with a loud raspberry.

Burgess continued to walk away, neither hearing nor caring. He was a quarter-mile away from the house. He felt good about himself. First time since he could remember. Anita was better looking now than at fifteen. Fuller. Meatier. He could make a fortune with her. He did not see the carriage pull up alongside, but his attention was once again focused as the driver hailed him down.

"Sir. If you please."

"Yeah?"

"The lady wishes to speak with you."

"What lady?"

The driver indicated his passenger, and Burgess refocused. He stood still for a moment, then walked over to the carriage.

"Yeah? What do you want, lady?"

"Get in. I would like to speak with you. I'll make it worth your while."

That was for him. Good looking woman with money. Now that he was a businessman, he should expect good fortune like this to come his way. He obeyed, and the carriage proceeded down the street, seeking out the gentler grades. The driver knew that he would be paid regardless of the route he chose, so there was no need to tire the horse climbing unnecessary hills.

Burgess recounted the story of Anita, J.J., Atherton, and himself. He relished telling the attractive lady what he and the Chinaman had in mind to bring Anita into line, but Anita was not cooperating. If the lady would help him, Burgess left no doubt of his future undying gratitude. He even suggested that the lady might well consider him for a lover herself.

Robin was silent, and fixed her gaze upon him, smiling, listening to his drivelogue, the clopping of the horse's hooves, and the grinding of the wheels into the street. What a disgusting piece of trash. A superb specimen of sewage, he was. A spent penis his only ambition. A full whiskey bottle his sole aspiration. A perfect match for Anita.

Morgan Farrington heard the footsteps approaching his office, and rose to answer the expected knock on the door.

"Come in," he responded.

Robin entered and Burgess followed.

"Are you Mr. Farrington?"

"Yes, Madam. Please come in. How do you do, Mister--?" Farrington's voice trailed upward, begging an answer.

"This is Mr. Burgess. Nathan Burgess. I am Mrs. Duchard. I would like to engage your services."

"Of course, Madam. Please sit down."

Robin explained the situation to Farrington as well as she understood it, given Burgess' incoherence. Burgess was a respected businessman, a partner of one Lin Thai-Saing. Anita was an impoverished indigent. Burgess wanted custody of J.J. and had no money. Robin had money and would pay for Farrington's services to obtain custody for Burgess. Could Farrington do it?

"I can request an application for custody. Just between us, I can persuade the court to grant custody to Mr. Burgess."

"How long will that take?"

"One week, Mrs. Duchard. Maybe two."

Robin reached into her purse for some twenty-dollar gold pieces. She began placing them on the desk, one at a time, accenting and punctuating her words.

"Justice should be done in a timely manner, don't you think so, Mr. Farrington?"

She looked deep into his eyes without wavering. How many coins would it take to make this leech come to life?

"What will it take to bring about timely justice for Mr. Burgess?"

Farrington's face brightened at the sight of the fourth coin. For that kind of money, he could pay the judge to issue the bench warrant in a day. In her estimation, therefore, he was a one hundred-dollar squire. She placed the fifth coin on the desk.

"Well, Mr. Farrington?"

"I'll have the bench warrant issued by tomorrow afternoon. In the interest of justice, of course, Mrs. Duchard."

"Thank you, Mr. Farrington. We must see justice done for Mr. Burgess. Our civic duty obliges us to do so."

"Indeed, Madam. Our civic duty," he mused as he picked up the coins.

Robin arose and offered her hand to Farrington. He stood, walked around the desk, took her hand, and kissed it.

"Madam."

"I must be leaving. Could you and Mr. Burgess complete the details?"

"Of course, Madam. And thank you."

"Good day, Mr. Burgess, and good fortune to you."

"Good day, Ma'am and thank you, Ma'am," replied Burgess, emulating their social amenities.

Burgess rose and reached for her hand. She ignored him, turned, and walked toward the door. Farrington opened it for her to exit and closed it behind her. She motioned to the waiting driver to help her into the carriage.

"March 11, 1855 ... Petitioner has acknowledged that he is the natural father of the illegitimate minor, John Jacob Travis, ... and custody is hereby granted to the Petitioner."

Bench Warrant, re Burgess v. Travis

Superior Court, San Francisco

"Go. Now. And don't ever come back."

Anita saw Reef walking toward the house. She began to cry. She had dreaded this moment. Now, she had to face him. She still loved him. She longed to hold him close to her, yet she did not want to look into his face.

He had dreaded the moment, too, and resolved to get it behind him with as much gentleness and sensitivity as he could muster. He walked up the steps, onto the porch, and entered the house.

"Hello, Anita."

"Hello, Reef."

"Robin came by?"

"Yes."

"Then, you know?"

"Yes."

"Anita," started Reef.

Anita wanted to contain her anger, but she could not. She interrupted and screamed at him.

"Why didn't you tell me? Why? Why did you lead me on?"

Reef was silent. He had not expected such a violent discharge of pent-up emotions, and he was not prepared to answer.

"How you must have laughed at me. How you made sport of me, and scolded me for keeping my baby a secret from you. How you must have laughed at me," she sobbed.

"No, that's not so. I didn't laugh. I didn't think things would go as far as they did. I didn't want you to be hurt."

"Well, I am hurt. You hurt me, and it cuts me deep. Oh, how deep it cuts into me."

Reef attempted to gather her into his arms.

"Anita."

Anita broke free and screamed at him again.

"Leave me alone. Don't put a hand on me. I'm not your plaything."

"No, you're not. I never treated you as one."

She calmed herself and lowered her voice.

"You'd better go, now. I'm sure you know the way to your wife's bedroom without any help. You don't belong here any more. Take the rest of your things and go."

"Anita."

She raised her voice in agony one final time, ending in a scream.

"Go. Now. And don't ever come back. Don't ever come back."

Anita left the room wailing, and slammed the door behind her. Reef fixed his eyes upon the closed door. A full minute passed. He walked over and entered his former bedroom.

All of his personal things, as well as those of the company, had been moved to the hotel. He picked up the few items that remained. A shot-riddled breastplate and a paper hat for Napoleon. A waybill fashioned into the shape of a feather. The remains of a board from a deserted shack. He put them down, and walked out of the room. Robin would neither understand nor appreciate them, and they had no place in his future. In the presence of suffering, he had learned long ago to turn and walk away.

He paced off the distance to the door, hoping that the one behind him would open before he could reach the one in front of him. Her door did not open. He left the house and walked out into the busy street. He did not remember walking back to the hotel, climbing the stairs and locking himself in the room.

An hour passed before Robin inserted her key in the lock, turned the bolt, and entered the room. Reef was sitting in the chair staring out the window, still depressed from his encounter with Anita. She sensed what was wrong. The time had come to offer him a prize, a sweetener, something to replace his morbid attachment to the street girl.

"Reef?"

"Yes?"

"I'm glad you're here. I have good tidings."

"What are they?"

"Father wants to finance you. Hire an agent to buy abandoned ships. Return to Boston, and run all of the Larimore shipping interests. Reef. He's offering you a full partnership."

Reef had not expected this. A full partnership in a bank. A man had to be fifty to even hope for such an offer. He was still eight years shy. He thought about the offer before he responded.

"That's a generous offer. I've always liked your father. I'll have to consider it carefully."

Robin was upset. What was there to think about? A full partnership in Larimore Bank, for crying out loud, and for doing next to nothing. Paul would pee in his pants to get such an offer.

"What do you mean? What is there to think about?"

Reef had seldom ever raised his voice to Robin. He did so now.

"I said I'd think about it. That ends it for now."

Robin froze. Had she made the offer in an abrupt manner? Or, had the little bitch pleaded with him? Worse yet, the tramp probably offered to be his mistress. The little trollop. Robin opted to leave Reef alone and let him think about it.

"Yes, dear. I'll be downstairs when you're ready for supper."

She left the room, turned the key in the lock, and went downstairs to the lobby.

"March 11, 1855 ... I ached to hold him. Instead, I sent him away. I just want to die."

Diary of Anita Travis

"She'll go with you to Utah ..."

Reef was alone in the office late, long after the last miner had left. Sutton had left thirty minutes before with his run of Exchange notes and dust bound for Panama. Only one run remained, the midnight treasure express by ferry to Oakland, and then by steamer to Sacramento. Reef was preparing his last run, loading newly minted gold coins into a treasure box, when a tapping on the shaded door interrupted him.

"Who's there?"

"Ellis Trowbridge. Please open the door."

Reef drew his pistol, full-cocked it, and opened the door wide enough to verify that Trowbridge was alone. He did not want some drunken miner coming in behind Trowbridge, with something to ship to a mother back home.

"Dr. Trowbridge."

"Mr. Atherton, please let us in. Quickly."

Reef opened the door wide. Trowbridge helped Caralina through the door and followed her, with his wives following in turn. Reef glanced up and down the street. He saw no one. He secured his pistol, then closed and locked the door behind them. They were dressed for travel and carried valises and carpetbags. Caralina was radiant in her new white dress and shoes and a green hooded cloak embroidered in gold. Reef was curious about her presence.

"How do you do, Mrs. Trowbridge? Mrs. Trowbridge? And Caralina. What is she doing here?"

"Mr. Atherton, I, we need your help," responded Trowbridge.

"What's the matter?"

"Thai-Saing is attempting to take Caralina back. I want to take her to Utah. She'll be safe there. We have no other place to go. We need your help."

"What happened? I thought this matter was settled."

"The court clerk is a Mormon. Out of kindness, he informed us that Thai-Saing paid off a judge to issue a bench warrant. For the return of a runaway slave. If the marshal serves the warrant, we'll lose her."

Reef was troubled by the news. What he had to do now bore hidden and perhaps unacceptable risks. Assisting a fugitive slave in avoiding arrest was a felony offense. A messenger represented the bank. If a messenger was caught breaking the law, the public trust would be shattered, and a run on the bank would result. The bank had just survived one panic and it did not need another.

Should he risk it? He stared at Trowbridge. He broke off the steady and unflinching gaze of the surgeon to focus upon Madelaine. No help there. Then, upon Beth Ellen. No help. Then, upon Caralina.

That was his undoing. Caralina lifted her chin and fixed her downcast eyes upon him. Her expression bore no plea, no supplication, no prayer. Only fear. Simple fear. Her eyes triggered in him a flood of memories of the larded black girl on the deck of the *Polar Star*, and the words of the mate,

"Go ahead, Atherton. Pick one to save."

Meeting her gaze was all that it took to convince him. Trowbridge had opened and Caralina had raised. Reef could either call or fold.

If he could save one, he would save this one.

He looked at the coin bags in the treasure box. He looked at packages in a trunk on the floor. He looked at Caralina again, comparing her size to the space in the trunk. He returned the contents of the treasure box to the safe, closed it, spun the dial, and then began emptying the trunk.

"Rummage for a blanket and pillows," ordered Reef, pointing Trowbridge toward the storeroom. He picked up Caralina and held her close to him. He was transfixed by her nearness. What an exquisite treasure she was. He loathed the thought of allowing her to return to the *Polar Star*. He vowed with silent resolve that he would not, as long as he had life within him. He kissed her on the forehead, and then on the nose.

She seemed to sense that this was goodbye. This was the man who had scolded her. This was the man who had stirred the memory of her father within her. He had tried to free her from the clutches of the miner, and had been beaten for his kindness. He had been angry with her, but he had been gentle, so unlike all the others.

Without warning, even as he lowered her into the trunk, she held his face in her hands and pressed her lips to his. Although many men had performed this ritual with her many times, for reasons unknown to her, this was the first time that she had ever initiated it. Or had ever wanted to. She whispered the words that she had spoken only to her father and mother so long ago.

"I love you."

Reef was moved by her declaration. He froze at her words. She was so close. She was so radiant. He yearned to prolong this precious encounter, but he could not. His sense of urgency forced him to ignore this private, final moment with her. His face softened, and it showed his appreciation for her kiss, but his voice was mindful of the task at hand.

"Make yourself as comfortable as possible. You'll be in here until the stage gets to Oakland, and perhaps beyond."

Trowbridge placed a blanket and two pillows in the trunk. Reef handed Caralina a flask of water and two apples. Trowbridge was puzzled.

"What are you doing?"

"I'm making a package out of her. A chattel. That way, a marshal can't search for her in here."

"Why not?"

"Because a fugitive slave warrant covers *persons* and not property. A marshal would have no reason to assume that a person is being shipped in a trunk that the company uses to ship *property*."

"Are you sure about this. What happens now?"

"Assign her bond to the company. That way, she becomes the *property* of Wells Fargo. A fugitive slave warrant will not allow him to search the trunk."

Reef took a waybill and started filling it out.

"Take your bond and assign her to Wells, Fargo and Company for the sum of one dollar."

"What?"

"Do as I say. We're almost out of time. I'll reassign her to you in Sacramento. Now do it."

"All right. I hope you know what you're doing."

"Me, too. Nobody will open this trunk but me. I will stay with her to Sacramento or beyond, as far as you feel it's necessary. Is that understood?"

"Understood. We're grateful, Mr. Atherton."

Reef picked up a cut-off shot gun when he heard the eleven-thirty stage coach pounding and grinding up to the station next door. The miners outside began gathering from the nearby saloons and lining up to pay for their passages. Reef motioned toward the trunk. Trowbridge lowered the lid, and Reef applied the lock.

"Help me with this, then go and get your passages and climb aboard the coach. I'll be in the rear boot with the trunk. Stay away from me, no matter what happens."

They took the trunk outside. Reef strapped the trunk to the rear boot of the stage, then returned to the office to douse the lamps. He closed and locked the iron doors, then climbed into the boot beside the trunk. Trowbridge was still not convinced, but he was at a loss to propose an alternate plan. He disappeared for a few minutes, paid for the tickets, then returned for one final request.

"Take care of her. Part of my family is in that trunk."

"No one will take her from me this time, doctor. She'll go with you to Utah, or I'll lie dead on the road. I give you my word."

"We're indebted to you, Mr. Atherton. I would be proud to present letters to my bishop on your behalf at any time."

"Letters? What kind of letters?"

"Why, to join our church, of course."

"To join your church?"

"Yes, sir. Any time."

"I don't know anything about praying, doctor."

Reef's remark silenced Trowbridge only for an instant or two, and the response was poignant.

"Neither did I. Until I learned."

Trowbridge shook Reef's hand, then climbed into the coach with his wives. The first whistle of the midnight ferry blew its mournful sound. At the sound of the third whistle, it would depart. The driver released the brakes, and the stage coach rolled away.

Reef stayed in the boot after the coach clattered onto the ferry. He studied each passenger as they walked by the coach. He spotted the city marshal at the same time that the marshal saw the coach. The marshal examined the passengers as they emptied the coach and then approached Trowbridge.

"Are you Dr. Ellis Trowbridge?"

"I am."

"I have a bench warrant for the return of the fugitive slave, Caralina Vestoni. Where is she?"

"See for yourself," responded Trowbridge, indicating the interior of the coach.

"She's not with me."

Reef was not troubled by the presence of the marshal, but seeing the four Chinamen watching the marshal heightened his sense of danger. Lin Thai-Saing was not leaving things to chance. He had brought Lin Wu and two of his floor guards to the ferry.

Reef heard the marshal open the door of the coach. The marshal looked inside, stepped onto the front wheel, and raised himself to examine the front boot. Satisfied that it was empty, he stepped down, then turned to the rear boot. Reef cocked both hammers, raised the shot gun off his lap, and rested it on his lame left forearm as the marshal spoke.

"What's in the box?"

"Company property," replied Reef.

"Would you mind opening it?"

"Can't. You'll have to get a search warrant, first."

"I have a bench warrant. For the return of the fugitive slave, Caralina Vestoni. Is she in there?"

"I can't help you. You'll need a search warrant to search this box."

"I can't get that kind of warrant this time of the morning. I have a bench warrant."

"That may be so, but I still can't help you."

"I can deputize some men and force you to open the box."

"I'm hired to protect the company's property. You know that. I'll kill anyone that tries to open this box. You know that, too."

It was a tense and silent pause for the two men. Facing two hammers at full-cock, the marshal had to conclude that Reef was committed and would not back down. The marshal decided that he had had enough.

"Calm down. Calm down. This matter can be settled peacefully. Will you swear that the trunk does not contain the subject of the bench warrant, Caralina Lucia Vestoni?"

"This box and its contents belong to Wells, Fargo and Company Express. You have my word on it."

The marshal was silent. Was that the proper answer to his question, or was he being deceived? The man had sworn. He was a banker, and a banker's word was his bond. Especially so, since this bank had survived the panic while others had failed. Therefore, the box contained property of the company, none of which was his business. The bank's business was not something sinister. Not something to die for.

"Well, that's good enough for me."

The marshal left the scene and the crowd disbanded, somewhat disappointed that there would be no shooting. Reef released the hammers. He returned to a more relaxed position, but the sight of Thai-Saing, Wu, and the guards on the wharf confirmed his opinion that the matter had not been resolved. Thai-Saing motioned for Wu and one floor guard to board the ferry. They obeyed without hesitation. Thai-Saing and the remaining guard waited until the ferry departed, and then disappeared into the crowd. The time on the ferry building clock was two minutes past midnight.

"March 12, 1855 ... Mr. Atherton risked his life to protect my beloved daughter.

*He asked for nothing in return. I will be
proud to sponsor him should the occasion
arise."*

> *Ellis Trowbridge*
> *Letter to Bishop Jennings Hartley*

" ... Welcome to Sacramento."

Wu and the floor guard avoided any direct
contact with the Trowbridges and the coach. They
avoided any move toward Reef and disappeared from
view. Reef moved his position from the bottom of the
boot to sit on top of the coach, allowing him a better
view and preventing anyone from surprising him from
underneath the coach or from his blind side.

From his perch, Reef could cover the rear of the
stage and both sides. He half-cocked both barrels
and waited, but he doubted that anyone would move
against him in public. He had to assume that their
orders were to kill him, which would make it easy to
snatch Caralina from the defenseless doctor.

He had to find a way to force their attack. He
could not be sure what they would do if he separated
from the Trowbridges, but it was the best course of
action. At the least, the doctor and his wives would
be out of danger. When the stage clattered off the

ferry, it rolled a few yards down the street to the stage office where Reef related his plan to the doctor.

"I'm taking the Sacramento steamer. You stay on the coach. Meet me at our office in Sacramento tomorrow morning."

"You think they'll try anything tonight?"

"We'll find out. At any rate, I think it's best this way."

"Then, I'll see you in Sacramento."

"Yes, you will."

Trowbridge returned to his wives and climbed into the coach while Reef hailed two wharf hands. The Sacramento steamer had waited for the ferry, and would leave soon, judging from the activity at its berth. Two long howls of the whistle confirmed his opinion. Reef wanted to get the trunk aboard, stowed with the cargo, far from any passengers. Wu and the guard would make their move in stealth and in darkness. He wanted to settle the issue while he was still wide-awake, so he paid for steerage, and let the aspiring miners have the premium passages and rooms on the well-lighted upper decks.

"Four bit load, need two backs over here," announced Reef at the few wharf hands still loafing about at this late hour. Two bits were a premium offer for loading baggage, and two hands scurried over.

"Aye Cap'n. We'll do a load for two bits apiece."

"This trunk is delicate. Put it aboard the steamer. No bumps, no scrapes, and each of you will get two bits. If you drop it, you go hungry."

The wharf hands lifted the trunk with unusual gentleness and followed Reef to the steamship office for ticketing. As requested, he was consigned to steerage, and the wharf hands followed him onto the steamer and turned aft toward the paddle wheel.

Reef chose a corner on the starboard deck that could be defended, facing the railing with the wheel at his back, the main deck to his left and less than ten feet of deck remaining to his right. He thanked the hands and paid them each a quarter dollar. They pocketed the coins, tipped their hats, and disappeared to find their next customers.

Before long, a third whistle signaled the wharf hands to raise the gangplank, and cast off the lines. The thrashing of the paddle wheel in the water filled Reef's ears and they were under way. Reef looked at his watch. In the dim light, he was able to make out the time of five minutes before one o'clock.

At twenty minutes past one o'clock in the morning, Reef saw the two shadows coming toward him in a casual manner. They walked together, then separated, then rejoined, and separated again, as if deciding the best way to approach their quarry. They reminded him of the sailors that he had watched in his youth. Shipmates of his, naked, hobbled, tied, trapping and raping the basted black girls on the decks of the *Polar Star*.

Chided for declining to participate in their game, he had been taught how to participate. He had learned how to enjoy it. Enjoy her. What did she call herself? *Iangala.* Was that really her name? Or something she had screamed while he was enjoying the throes of passion? That name had not been on his mind or on his lips in thirty years. He had learned how to turn and walk away from suffering. He had learned how to be a man. What is different this time? Why is Caralina any different? Because she is white?

He could not answer his own questions, but he was no longer a helpless boy, and he vowed that the outcome of this game would be different. He cocked both hammers on the shot gun, confident of the damage that it would wreak. He had decided. He was not going to wait until he was attacked. He would not be tossed in the skysail this night.

The guard turned, sauntered into the darkness, and loitered near Reef's left side, facing him. Wu continued strolling toward the railing, acting casual, gazing out into the river, ignoring Reef, but ready to turn and attack. Wu would take a little more time to pass Reef before reaching his position, so the best choice was to shoot the waiting guard while Wu was still enjoying his stroll.

It was murder and Reef knew it. They had not made clear any intention to take possession of the trunk or to try him for it. He would have to lie in his report. He no longer cared. If any witness could accuse him of murder, then he would stand accused. For Caralina, he would commit murder.

His forefinger squeezed the left trigger. His persistence with his shot gun experiments had paid off and he was validated. The torso of the guard was blown completely open, scattering his bones and lungs over the bulkheads and onto the deck behind him. The loud discharge aroused screams from distant passengers.

Reef took advantage of the expected recoil to turn the gun in an instant and point it at Wu's stomach. Wu raised his hands. Despite the intended surrender, Reef shouted his indictment and his intent to free his precious treasure from their vicious claws.

"Carrion eater. This time, I jumped your claim. She's mine now."

Even as Wu began to back away, Reef reduced the odds once more. The force of the blast blew Thai-Saing's bodyguard and most of his ribs and intestines backward, over and through the railing, and into the water. Without hesitation, Reef pulled his Colt, full-cocked it, and laid it on the trunk while he began to reload the shot gun.

A crowd was forming with caution, examining the dead body of the guard and spreading an alarm to other passengers. Two of the women began to cry. Another leaned over the rail and vomited.

The captain rushed upon the scene and pushed his way through the crowd. After surveying the damage, he decided upon a judicious and expedient course of action. He barked orders to deck hands to drag the remains to the side and cover them with a tarpaulin. Since there was no law officer aboard, and no satisfactory way to determine who had jurisdiction, the captain elected to continue the journey and report the incident to the Sacramento authorities with whatever details he could gather.

"This man try to rob you?"

"Yes," replied Reef. "My name is Atherton. I'm a messenger. You can get statements from the two gentlemen behind you and from the lady at the railing. They may have seen what happened."

"All right, Mr. Atherton," replied the captain. "I'll log this and have you speak with the sheriff in Sacramento."

"I have perishable express here. For delivery to the Wells Fargo office. Have the sheriff come over there."

The captain agreed. Two deck hands appeared with mops and a tarpaulin. Cleaning up the gore consisted of using the mops to push the blood and pieces of flesh and bone across the promenade through the railing and over the side, then dip the mop in the river, wring it out, and repeat the process. When they were finished mopping, they covered the corpse and left the scene. By the time this was accomplished, the captain had obtained his sworn statements.

Reef was alone. The sole sound was the unending sloshing of the paddle wheel in the water. No sound issued from the trunk, so Reef tapped on the lid.

"Hey, little one. Are you awake?"

"Yes, Mr. Atherton, I'm awake. What happened?"

"Just some Chinese fireworks. Giving you a proper welcome to Sacramento. Can you stay in there a little while?"

"Yes, sir. I'm fine in here."

"Good. Try to sleep. I'll be here if you need me."

Reef finished reloading, returned his Colt to its holster, settled in, and prepared to continue his watch for the balance of the night. He glanced at the covered corpse. Thai-Saing would no doubt come after him now. He sucked a mouthful of mucus into his mouth and spat it upon the covered remains of the dead guard.

"Please, Nathan. Don't do this to me."

A loud knock on the door interrupted Anita's afternoon nap. J.J. remained asleep beside her, but he was beginning to stir. She eased herself off the bed and tiptoed out of the bedroom in the hopes of prolonging his nap. She crossed the living room and opened the front door to face the city marshal. He stood alone with a bench warrant in his hand.

"You Anita Travis?"

"Yes."

"You have a son, John Jacob?"

"Yes. What's the matter?"

"Where is he? I have a warrant to pick him up."

"Why? What has he done?"

"Nuthin', ma'am. Court wants him to be with the father, what with him being a businessman, and you being, well, you understand."

"No. I don't understand. You can't take him. He's mine, and he's all I have."

"I'm sorry, ma'am. I'm no judge, and I didn't issue the warrant. I just have to serve it. Now, where is he?"

J.J. appeared at the door, jostling his mother. The marshal was quick to grab him before Anita could warn the boy or protest any further. Anita screamed and began to cry, clutching at the marshal with one hand, and at J.J. with the other. J.J. screamed and kicked, but was unable to free himself.

"Mommy, make him let me go."

"No. Please, don't. Don't do this."

She followed the marshal to his wagon, screaming and begging for J.J.'s release. Burgess was in the wagon, enjoying Anita's anguish. He took J.J. from the marshal, as Anita pleaded with him.

"Please, Nathan. Don't do this to me. Don't do this to me."

"You behave proper, Anita. You can see J.J. after you talk with Mr. Lin."

Anita screamed at the sound of Lin Thai-Saing's name, and tried to retrieve the boy. Burgess pushed her away with his boot, and she fell to the ground, sobbing.

"He wants to talk to you, first. You be reasonable. You work for me and earn your keep, like I asked you before."

The marshal had no intention of interfering in a domestic squabble. He pretended not to notice, climbed in the wagon, and drove the three of them down the street toward the *Polar Star*.

"March 14, 1855 ... Re: John Jacob Travis, a minor, the Bench Warrant was served and has been satisfied."

Clerk of the Superior Court,
City of San Francisco

"This is my last run ..."

Reef stirred up a commotion in the Sacramento office when he inserted the barrel key into the lock and a sleepy young girl emerged from the trunk. Fewer than a dozen miners were in the office to witness the incident, but hundreds swore later that they had personally witnessed the marvelous event. The news spread in a day throughout Sacramento and the miner's word-of-mouth telegraph shouted it from claim to claim into the hills.

Since Reef anticipated no further threat from Lin Thai-Saing and his men, he bid the girl and the Trowbridges a sad goodbye as the stage coach left the Sacramento office. He told them of his plans to return to Boston, so they knew that this was the last time that they would be together.

The news of the girl in the trunk gave instant credence to the spreading belief that the company would and could deliver anything and anyone just about anywhere. The story was relished and embellished on its way through the hills and valleys of the Sierras. Passing from miner to merchant, merchant to drummer, along the roads, the rivers, and their tributaries, the story of the little girl and her pursuers traveled faster than the Concord coach that bounced and rocked the Trowbridges on their way to Utah.

It happened at Roseville. Then, at Auburn. Again at Grass Valley, and again at Nevada City. Miners bathed. They shaved. They unpacked their last white shirt and washed it. They unpacked or bought up every last long coat, top hat, and cravat between Sacramento and Reno.

They left their claims and their swollen creek beds for as long as it took to climb to the nearest road as the pounding of hooves and the grinding of wheels heralded the passing of the coach. Just to get a glimpse of a little girl with raven black hair clothed in a white dress and green-and-gold hooded cape, and to wave to her as the horses galloped by.

The girl had achieved a measure of celebrity. At each stop of the stage coach to rest the passengers or change the horses, a crowd formed to greet her. She did not know why she warranted the attention, but to show her gratitude she gave each impromptu audience a most welcome and well-received rendition of a song or an aria taught to her by her beloved mother. Her enroute performances increased her popularity and further expanded her legend.

In San Francisco, she had been an obscure harlot. In Sacramento, she was promoted to sweetheart. By the time she reached Grass Valley, she had been crowned a princess, and by Reno, consecrated to the rank of an angel. No longer in a trunk, she traveled inside the stage coach with the special messenger that Reef had assigned as an escort to Salt Lake City.

Now that the Caralina matter was ended, Reef had other matters on his mind -- to get Robin aboard a ship for protection, and settle accounts with Thai-Saing. A treasure run to San Francisco was ever ready for shipment on the steamer that night, and the previous night's events had left him in need of some rest. The mattress and pillow in the storeroom felt like goose down to him, as he ignored the lumps of cotton stuffing, the smell of dried sweat, and the sag in the rope lashings of the cot.

"Wake me an hour before the steamer leaves," was Reef's final request to the agent.

"I want to be on that boat. This is my last run and then, I'm on my way home to Boston."

Home to Boston. He had been away from home for almost two years. Now, as a full partner at Larimore's Bank, he could stay at home and pay agents to do the work in San Francisco.

The formula was simple. Give up the *Polar Star*. The legal battle to reclaim it was pointless, since it was landlocked forever. Hire skilled riggers and sailmakers to refit the best of hundreds of other abandoned ships already floating in the Bay of San Francisco. Ship owners would pay a handsome sum for the return of their ships to the profitable trade routes. For those who could not pay, he would take a percentage of ownership. For those who refused to pay, he would have their ships condemned as *Public Annoyances*, and his agents would buy them at auction for pennies on the dollar just as Thai-Saing had done. Here was a niche, a trail that he could follow, and a path to great wealth. He slept without stirring until an arriving steamer's whistle awakened him for his final run.

Tonight, he was escorting gold dust with a value in the thousands of dollars. What a difference from the previous night, when he was guarding a little girl that he had purchased for one dollar. He smiled to himself. How little an appraised value he had placed upon the waybill for such a precious treasure.

He verified the contents of the treasure box and signed for the amount on the waybill, fifty-four thousand dollars. Two wharf hands were waiting at the counter to transport the treasure box to the waiting steamer one block away. The night run was expected and prepaid by the agent at the commutation rate, so Reef did not have to stop to purchase a passage. This would be a "milk run," a first class passage, with a space for the treasure box, reminding him of Carson's grip bag on the Boston to New York train so many lifetimes ago.

In the morning, Carson would be at the office to greet him, congratulate, laugh, reminisce with him, and bid him farewell. A single thought remained. He would miss the company of the men with whom he had shared so many days and nights in the offices and along the roads to the distant camps.

> *"March 15, 1855 ... Rec'd for shipment 225 pounds gold dust @ $20, value $54,000, Sacto to SF."*
> *Twelve*
> *Receipt for Treasure*
> *W.F. & Co. Ex.*

"Please, Mr. Lin. Can I go home and bathe?"

Anita composed herself to cover her grief. She stopped crying as she knocked on the door of the captain's quarters of the *Polar Star*. She dried her eyes with a handkerchief and prepared herself for the abuse that she was facing.

A floor guard opened the door and let her in. He took his exit to stand guard outside and closed the door behind him. Lin Thai-Saing rose to greet her.

"Come in, my sweet child. I am so happy that you see fit to grace my chambers."

"Yes, sir."

He placed his hands on her cheeks and then wiped away a remaining tear.

"So unhappy. Dry your beautiful eyes, my love. Let me see no tears in Anita's eyes again. They make your face so salty, so dirty. Reach into your heart. Let it present a smile to your face, instead. A pretty smile. For Lin Thai-Saing."

"Yes, Mr. Lin. May I see my baby, now?"

"You want to see your son. That is good. Babies belong with their mothers. I will let you see your son, but first, you must do something for Lin Thai-Saing."

He took her by the hand and led her to his bed. Sitting down, he pulled her down beside him. She knew what he was about to do.

"What do you want me to do?"

"You will sing your love song for Lin Thai-Saing. Here. Now."

He forced a kiss, the smell and taste of which disgusted her. She started to resist, but relented, knowing that a show of resistance would place her mission in jeopardy. She surrendered to his kiss, keeping her teeth together and her eyes closed. She began to cry.

Thai-Saing was not about to be insulted or put off by the girl. She was in no position to refuse and he knew it. Rather than anger, he chose to play with her.

"Be Lin Thai-Saing's love. Bond yourself to me. Here. Now. Then, you will see your son. Any time you wish."

He kissed her again. She resisted this time and broke free, sobbing.

"How can I believe you? Can I see J.J., now? Just for a minute? Please?"

Thai-Saing was annoyed at the delay, but what difference would a few more minutes make?

"Then, come."

He lead her to a peephole into the first mate's quarters and opened it. She stood on her tiptoes and peered inside. Burgess was lying nude across a bunk, passed out beside a naked sing-song girl. Anita felt like vomiting.

"That's Nathan."

"Look again. By the chair."

Anita gasped and froze in horror. J.J. was playing on the floor, oblivious to the sleeping couple and unaware of his mother's presence. Thai-Saing closed the peephole, and Anita fought to hold back her tears. He walked over to the desk and picked up a *Bond of Indenture*. Her name was on it. He walked back to her and rubbed her neck, chin, cheek, and lips with it. He unbuttoned the collar of her dress and placed it inside. He took her hand, and led her to his desk. He picked up a pen, opened a bottle of ink, dipped the pen in the ink, and handed it to her.

"You see? Your son is in good hands. Lin Thai-Saing will take good care of him and you. You will sing your love song for me now. See your son afterwards."

Anita was distraught. What could she do?

Is my life, my love, worth no more than this? A whore in the Polar Star? Three-pinches of gold? Four? Five? Nights with a drunken miners. Mean sailors. I need time to think. I have to get out of here. What can I do? Oh, God, what can I do?

"Please, Mr. Lin. Can I go home and bathe? Please? And put on a pretty dress for you? And wash my face? I feel dirty. And my gold. I want to get my gold."

Thai-Saing reacted to her reference to the precious metal.

"Gold?"

"Yes, Mr. Lin. I saved it for J.J.'s schooling. It needs safekeeping. I hid it at home, and I don't want to leave it there."

Lin Thai-Saing was aroused and eager to rape the girl. Her screams would be drowned out by the din of the saloon. The only obstacle in his path now was this conflict of interest between competing lusts. This was too good to pass up. Gold. Free for the taking. With misgivings and reluctance, he put down the pen.

"Gold. Yes. I will keep it for your son. Go and get your gold and make yourself pretty for me. When you return, you will sing your love song for Lin Thai-Saing in this bed. Then, you will see your son. Do you understand?"

"Yes, Mr. Lin. I understand."

Anita was relieved. At least she would have time to prepare herself for the inevitable horror of subjecting herself to Thai-Saing's demands and those of her future customers. Perhaps she would kill herself, instead. Perhaps she would take the gold, run away, and take the steamer to Sacramento or Los Angeles.

Lin Thai-Saing removed the bond from her dress with deliberate delay, toyed with her again, then escorted her to the door. As she started to exit, he barred her way, pulled her to him, and forced another long and wet kiss. She dared not register her disgust. She closed her eyes and her mouth, and offered no response, negative or otherwise. She allowed him to indulge himself, hoping that he would not change his mind.

He did not. The lure of gold was enough to make him wait a little longer to vent his aching for her. What a windfall, and what a prize she would be. He parted his mouth from her lips, looked at her, and reflected upon the words that he would say to her when she returned with the gold. For fear of scaring the girl, he did not speak them aloud.

"I have watched you and wanted you. You are almost a virgin. Only one coupling at fifteen and no man for five years. Tonight, on your *first night* of love, with me alone, I will loosen all of the ties that bind up your desires. I will rekindle the flame within you one tense moment to the next, and the next, and we will spend the entire night quenching it."

The floor guard was standing by the door. He turned to see his master smile at him, point to him, and then point to Anita. He understood. He watched his master toy with the girl, then smiled in anticipation of his own *second night* with her. He would not have her the entire night, and it would be at the discretion of Thai-Saing, but he was a loyal guard, and he had just been notified that he was deserving of the master's gratuity.

Thai-Saing completed his fantasy.

"The righteous shopkeepers and merchants along the streets all know you. They will line up out the door to bid for you on your *virgin night*. You will perform for them, from the highest bidder on down, while the rest of us drink, sing, and applaud."

He kissed her again and released her. Anita fled from the room and the groping hands of Thai-Saing and the guard.

"March 16, 1855 ... Mr. Lin has taken my sweet baby away from me. To see my darling boy again, to hold him and kiss him is all that I have to live for now."
        Diary of Anita Travis

"Forgive me if I troubled you ..."

Her tears formed and tried to escape from her eyes. Anita restrained them and continued to brush her hair. She tied it with a ribbon and rouged her cheeks and her lips. This was no time for tears. This was her first night as a working girl, and for working girls, there could be no room for tears.

Perhaps this way was best. Reef was gone from her life, back to Boston with Robin. At least, he would not have to witness what was going to happen to her. She stood for a final inspection, approved of her professional presentation, picked up her purse, bulging with its treasure, and prepared to go out the door.

As an afterthought, she picked up her diary, opened it, and pieced together the torn parchment. She read for the last time the intimate thoughts that she had penned, when was it, one hundred years ago? She paused. Her poem needed a final farewell, but not to Nathan. This was for her beloved Reef, words that he would never see.

Tell him that you miss him. Tell him you know that you can never have him.

> *"So now, I go my way alone,*
> *'Today' is calling me again.*
> *Allow me this, my childhood love,*
> *I long to hold you once again."*

Remember, he did not like poetry. Ask his forgiveness and say goodbye, and tell him how you feel about him now.

> *"Forgive me if I troubled you,*
> *Farewell my love, I had to know.*
> *Forgive me, I no longer cry.*
> *I know I cannot let you go."*

She reshuffled the pieces, returned them to the diary, and put it away in the drawer. After one long, last look around, she blew out the lamp, left the room, and closed the door.

The streets were almost empty of people and wagons going to and from the docks at that time of the morning. She had to hurry. That-Saing wanted her at the *Polar Star* no later than two o'clock. She held her head down, not wanting to look into the faces of the pedestrians, or to acknowledge any one of the many merchants that she knew. She faced a disgusting physical performance tonight, one for which they would soon revile her, and she did not want to be distracted by an exchange of meaningless pleasantries.

At the entrance of the *Polar Star*, she was stopped by the floor guard.

"What do you want?"

"My name is Anita. I have come to see Mr. Lin. Is he here"

The guard examined her face and figure. He leered and grinned.

"Good ship, *Polar Star*. You made the right choice. You be my steady girl and I take care of you. No harm come to you. You'll see."

"I must see Mr. Lin. Is he here?"

The guard pointed toward the bow of the ship.

"He's outside, at the other end of the house. Come inside with me. I'll show you around until he returns."

Anita declined.

"No, thank you. I'll find him myself."

She turned and walked toward the passageway between the ships and along the path that would take here to the bow of the *Polar Star*.

"March 16, 1855 ... Tonight, I will shame myself and my family. I will pretend not to care anymore, so I can have my baby again."

                  Diary of Anita Travis

"My song has only one note."

At ten minutes before two in the morning, Reef was running late. The note that had been delivered to the hotel had read,

"The girl and her son for the gold.
Bow of the *Polar Star* at two."

To Reef, the meaning was clear enough. Thai-Saing wanted his gold returned, or Anita and J.J. would be floating in the bay in the morning.

Reef was anxious to get Robin aboard the ship and excuse himself for his alleged "last minute duties." She would be safe there. She could refresh herself, unpack, and claim the most comfortable accommodations ahead of the other passengers that would board later that morning. His plan was simple. Settle the matter with Thai-Saing and return to the ship.

Other passengers, mostly miners returning home with bags of gold dust, would be bargaining for the common vacancies, but Robin was looking forward to establishing her preference for a cabin next to the captain's quarters, one that would be both private and comfortable.

She was enthusiastic about the voyage and was eager to depart forever the dirty and morbid surroundings and her depressing memories of San Francisco town.

"Father will be so happy to see you again. He's so pleased with your plans to buy the ships. Since you've been gone, all the ship owners are buying steamers, and gouging the shippers. Well, you know more about that than I do, Reef. Reef, are you listening to me?"

Reef paid her proper lip service as he paid the hack driver and hired a porter to take their luggage down the dock to the waiting ship.

"Yes, I'm listening. Yes, I'll be glad to be home again. What's that you said about your father?"

"Reef, you weren't listening."

"Robin, get aboard and have the captain let you pick out some comfortable quarters. I have some last-minute details to attend."

He turned and started down the starboard passageway to the bow of the *Polar Star*.

Lin Thai-Saing was waiting in the darkness between the bow of the *Polar Star* and its landlocked neighbors. Burgess was standing at a distance, holding J.J. by the hand. Two guards crouched behind crated cargoes, eager for the first opportunity to kill Reef.

Anita approached Lin Thai-Saing from the deserted and unlighted port passageway. When he saw her, he motioned to those behind him to be silent, for she had not seen the others. The two were alone. She approached Thai-Saing and managed to address him with a soft tone.

"Do you like my dress, Mr. Lin? I have bathed for you. I have my gold, and I will sing my love song for you, if you will let me see my baby."

"You are lovely my dear. And there is your son, like I promised."

He turned, stepped aside, and indicated the presence of the child and Burgess a short distance away. J.J. saw his mother and started to run to her, but Burgess held him fast.

"Mommy."

"J.J.," screamed Anita.

Thai-Saing grabbed Anita's arm, held her back, and grinned. She smelled of clean hair and clothes, and he was aroused by her presence.

"First, my flower, you will grace the chambers of Lin Thai-Saing."

The light in his wide eyes matched that of the grin on his face.

"But first, give me the gold."

Anita turned to him as he reached for her heavy purse. He was a man obsessed, and anxious to grasp the gold coins within it. Her time to perform was upon her, and she took the cue, passing the heavy purse to him.

Thai-Saing felt with a rare sense of glee the clinking of the gold coins, as he removed the purse from her grasp. He was not aware that his act of acquisition was also removing Anita's makeshift holster from the Colt that Reef had given her. The pistol emerged from the purse at half-cock. A grim determination and a look of calm flowed into Anita's face as she full-cocked the pistol with the smooth motion that Reef had taught her, and pointed it at Lin Thai-Saing's heart.

"My song has only one note, my love. And I sing it to you."

She pulled the trigger in one smooth motion, and the machine performed precisely as it was designed. The loud explosion echoed along the passageway, and Thai-Saing was thrown back against the hull of the *Polar Star*. A look of shock came over him. Disbelieving, he dropped to his knees. He was dead. Anita grabbed her purse and stepped aside. His face followed his blood into the street. The guards were stunned. They had watched their master die. Facing the girl and her smoking pistol, they cancelled their allegiance to their dead master and retreated into the night. Burgess was frozen with terror as Anita turned his way.

Reef had heard the shot. He warned Robin as he moved toward the sound.

"Stay aboard. You'll be safe there. I have to go."

Robin had no intention of staying behind. Whatever was happening, she wanted to be a witness, especially where her newly reclaimed husband was concerned. Reef rushed down the starboard passageway to the bow of the *Polar Star*. He saw Anita facing Burgess and heard J.J.'s plea.

"Mommy."

J.J. tried to run to her, but again Burgess held him. Reef stopped short. Then, J.J. saw Reef and screamed again.

"Mr. Reef. Mr. Reef."

Burgess was stunned to see Reef and loosened his grip on J.J. The boy seized the opportunity, wrestled free, and ran toward Reef. Then Burgess saw Robin.

That bitch. He lost his temper, drew his pistol, and screamed at her.

"You bitch. You double-crossing bitch."

Robin had caught up to Reef. At the sight of Burgess, and upon hearing his curse, she felt a chill of terror. Reef pushed her out of the way behind bales of hides, and reached for his pistol as J.J. came up to him and grabbed his legs.

Reef had only the right arm that was capable of both defending himself and pulling J.J. out of the line of fire. The possibility that the child could take a ball in the back was abhorrent to him. He abandoned his reach for his Colt and grabbed the boy by his coat with his right hand and left arm, hoisting him high and away from him, tossing him behind the hides that shielded Robin. J.J. landed on the woman, knocking her down. He was safe for the moment.

Reef had no time to reach for his weapon. He was unable to recover from J.J.'s distraction and face Burgess. The sound of Burgess' shot roared down the passageway and the ball ripped into Reef's chest and knocked him off his feet and into the dirt with a force that knocked the wind out of him. The half-drawn pistol in Reef's crippled left hand went flying into the dirt as Burgess cocked his pistol and started toward Robin.

Anita was not finished. She brought her hammer to the full-cock position and her aim was accurate. The shot from her pistol tore into Burgess' neck and he went down squirting blood. J.J. freed himself from Robin's grasp and emerged from the bale of hides to find his mother.

"Mommy."

Anita dropped the pistol beside the dying Burgess, and ran to J.J. Robin saw that her husband was crawling toward Burgess and was afraid of what the madman might do to Reef.

"Someone. Help us," she yelled.

A crowd had formed, as one always did when a shooting occurred, not so much as to provide assistance, but more to gaze upon the faces of Burgess and the infamous Lin Thai-Saing. Reef was still dazed and was having trouble regaining his wind. He crawled over to the dying Burgess and heard his final lament.

"That Duchard bitch. She double-crossed me. For you? Atherton? You get her, too? Atherton? Huh? You're shit, Atherton. I won't miss. Next time. I won't miss. Ather--"

Burgess coughed up blood and exhaled a final long breath as the city marshal came running to the scene of death. He examined the two bodies for signs of life. He found none. He was serious and said little. He was performing a rather mundane, ordinary, and routine duty.

"What happened?"

Reef was still gasping for air, dazed on the ground. He felt an intense pain in the chest and now realized that Burgess had shot him. He reached inside his coat to stop the blood. The ball had torn his coat, but his hand could feel no blood. He felt into his coat pocket. His fingers touched pieces of the *Union* case and the remains of a destroyed daguerreotype. He looked up to see Robin bent over him.

"Reef. Are you hurt?"

Reef was still confused. He pulled himself to a sitting position. His vision was blurred, but he was coherent.

"Your dogtype. Robin. Your dogtype. It's gone."

"You're not hurt, are you Reef? Are you hurt?"

By now, the frustrated city marshal was looking for someone to respond.

"I said, what happened?"

This was the slap in the face that awakened Reef. He grasped the seriousness of the moment. Anita had just murdered two men in cold blood. Reef knew that men did not take lightly women using guns, or much less, committing murder. This crowd could become a mob with very little provocation. The city marshal would not be able to stop them. They would hang her without a trial with J.J. watching. He had to intervene. He collected his wits and enough strength to stand and respond.

"You know me. I'm with the Express Office. Montgomery Street. They tried to rob me, so I shot them. Arrest them both."

The marshal picked up Anita's pistol.

"Yes, I remember you. Is this the Chinaman's?"

"Messenger Hodges gave it to me. Arrest them."

"They're both dead. Were you a messenger? Guarding treasure again?"

"Yes."

"I don't see any treasure. I'll need a witness. Did anyone witness this?"

"I don't know. I don't think so."

The marshal turned to the crowd.

"Did anyone witness this?"

The crowd was silent. Even if they had witnessed the shooting, no man wanted to admit it.

The coroner's inquest would infringe upon their mining, drinking, and whoring. Only Anita and Reef knew the truth. They looked at each other as the marshal continued to investigate.

"Two dead by your hand. No treasure. No witnesses. That's too bad for you. You'll have to come with me."

Tong Wen-How stepped forward from the crowd, allowing a poke filled with gold coins to fall at his feet.

"Mr. marshal. Is this what you seek?"

"Who are you?"

"I am Tong Wen-How, from the neighborhood above Montgomery Street."

"What did you see?"

"The messenger speaks the truth. These men tried to rob him of his treasure. Perhaps this is what you are seeking," again indicating the gold at his feet.

The marshal stooped over to pick it up. He looked at the dead men. He looked at Reef. He thought for a moment. He looked at Tong Wen-How. Chinamen always perplexed him. You never could tell what they were thinking, and they never answered your question with the answer that you expected.

"The messenger speaks the truth," was the answer you got, and by then you couldn't even remember the question that you had asked, but you were dead certain it wasn't "Did this messenger speak the truth?"

Frustrated, he handed the gold poke and the pistol to Reef, and began dragging Burgess out of the dark passageway and into the light.

"All right, you have a witness, but you both will have to attend the inquest. What's your name and where do you live?"

"Atherton. I was staying at the Barclay Hotel, but I'm sailing for Boston this morning."

"You'll have to take the next ship. Come to the courthouse around noon. You can talk to the coroner then, and you can testify, but right now, I've got to get these remains to the morgue."

As the marshal departed, Anita put J.J. down, held his hand, and walked over to Reef and Robin.

"Thank you for what you did. Thank you for giving me back my baby. That's twice, isn't it?"

She hugged and kissed Reef on each cheek and the mouth, and with tears in her eyes, she ignored Robin, turned, and walked away with the boy. Reef looked after her. The steamer's whistle gave one long mournful howl, reminding Reef that he would not be on it that night.

Robin was incensed by the touching scene, and resented being relegated to a minor position. She tugged at his sleeve to restore his attention to her.

"Let's go back to the hotel. One more night in this pigsty is about all I can stand."

Reef kept picking pieces of the *Union* case out of his coat pocket as they walked toward the hotel. He was troubled. Something was not right.

"March 16, 1855 ... I shot Mr. Lin and Nathan tonight. I know I have committed a grave sin, but I will not repent, for I am not sorry. May God damn their dirty souls to Hell."

Diary of Anita Travis

"I missed you."

The coroner's inquest was a cold and lifeless legal action, sworn to by all present, and carried out in a cold and lifeless courtroom, borrowed for the morning by the coroner, his clerk, twelve jurors, the witnesses, and the city marshal. The purpose of the inquest was to

> *"... inquire in what manner, when, and how the deceased came to meet his death, who he was, and into all the circumstances attending such death; and to make a true inquisition according to the evidence or arising from the investigation of the body."*

The first inquest was held for Burgess, an indigent white man, and the action was identical for Lin Thai-Saing, as recorded by the clerk. The coroner spoke at large.

"Name, age, occupation, and residence of the deceased."

"Lin Thai-Saing, about 40, owner of the *Polar Star* brothel. That is his residence." responded the marshal.

"Cause of death?"

"Gunshot wound to the heart."

"By whose hand?"

"Reef Atherton, express messenger, here present," perjured Reef.

"Circumstances?"

"Attempted robbery," responded Reef.

"Do you have any witnesses?"

"Tong Wen-How, a Chinaman," responded the marshal.

"I am Tong Wen-How, honorable judge."

"Is this true? Was this an attempted robbery?"

"Mr. Atherton was protecting his treasure."

There was another Chinese answer for you, thought the marshal. He knew better than to interrupt the action and try to pin the Chinaman down as to exactly what happened. Two more inquests were on the docket and by nightfall probably a couple more corpses. To hell with it.

"Enter a decree of excusable homicide," the coroner indicated to the clerk.

"Case closed. You are free to go, Mr. Atherton, Mr. Tong. Next case."

Outside the courtroom, Reef thanked Tong, returned the gold coins to him, and bid him a grateful farewell.

"I owe you a great debt, Mr. Tong. One that I fear I can never repay."

"Friends do not tally debt, Mr. Atherton. Only time spent together."

Tong handed Reef the pistol that he had lost in the dirt the night before. It was clean and smelled of fresh oil.

"How did you know, Mr. Tong?"

"How did I know what?"

"How did you know to be at the bow of the *Polar Star* at two o'clock in the morning?"

"I received a note."

"Thai-Saing sent you a note?"

"I am not permitted to say who sent it, but it was not Mr. Lin."

"Goodbye, Mr. Tong."

"Have a good voyage, Mr. Atherton, to whatever destination you travel."

Reef was still troubled. He spent part of the afternoon at the Bank saying goodbye to his associates. Something was not right. He walked down to the wharf to obtain passage for himself and Robin on a steamer that would leave for Panama that night. He passed the *Polar Star*. Shu-Chuan was outside with her girls. She was dressed in white mourning garb. She saw him and motioned to him. He walked over to her and she bowed to him.

"I have something for you. Please wait here."

She disappeared into the *Polar Star*. Reef had never met her and he was apprehensive. He prepared to draw his pistol if she returned with guards. She did not. She came over to him with two girls and handed him a bundle.

"This belongs to you."

She bowed, motioned to her girls to follow her, and then returned to the brothel.

In his hands were books wrapped in a black silk cover. The logbooks of the *Polar Star* were an unexpected gift from the dead slaver's wife. She had read the books. She knew who he was. She had been privy to all of Thai-Saing's schemes and machinations. Reef understood. She had been dispatched with one note to the Barclay Hotel. She had written another and had taken it to a well-known leader of the Chinese community. Tong Wen-How. What manner of woman was this who would betray her husband to help total strangers?

Reef hired a hack, climbed in, and leafed through the books as he returned to the Barclay Hotel.

Robin and Reef packed their bags and he arranged for their belongings to be carted to the ship. After supper, he hired another hack, and they proceeded to the docks. Boarding had begun, and Robin spotted her trunks.

"They're porting my baggage aboard, Reef. Yours will be next, I trust."

Robin was eager to leave behind her forever this dirty town, the little slut Anita, this ludicrous excuse for a Bank, and California in general.

"It'll be so good to see Mother, Father, and Paul again, don't you think?"

Paul.

Reef had not heard that name in two years.

Paul.

Paul Duchard.

Duchard.

That Duchard bitch. Those were the words of the dying Burgess. Reef reached into his coat pocket and retrieved the remains of the gold filigree matting and the dogtype. He stared at the remains of Robin's image. Robin sensed that something was bothering Reef.

"Reef. What's wrong?"

"I'm not going with you, Robin."

"Not going with me? What do you mean, not going with me? Reef Atherton, get on board this instant. We're going back to Boston, where we belong. We're married. We belong to each other."

"No, Robin. We're finished. I'm staying."

"What are you talking about?"

"Burgess called you 'Duchard,' Robin. 'That Duchard bitch.' He was going to shoot you, Robin. How did he know you? And why would he think your name was Duchard?"

Robin had been exposed. She was silent. She was scared. Reef continued.

"And the rouge."

"What?"

"The rouge. Anita never paints her face with rouge."

"So?"

"She was going to work for Thai-Saing, wasn't she?"

"Well, how would I know what the little trollop was planning to do?"

"From Burgess."

"What do you mean?"

"Burgess. He wasn't screaming at Anita. He was screaming at you. He thought you double-crossed him, not Anita."

"You're delirious."

"You fixed it for him, didn't you Robin? Somehow, you fixed it so Anita would have to work for him and Thai-Saing. That's how he knew you. You told him your name was Duchard."

Robin had to face the truth. Reef had uncovered her betrayal, and she was losing him. She had to think of something. Fill the interim. Cry.

"No, Reef. That's cruel of you to say those things to me."

"Go home to Paul, Robin."

"Paul? He's just a friend. He lost everything in the panic. He has no way to recover from it."

"I'm sorry for him, Robin. And for you. But that doesn't change anything. I'm staying here."

She was not convincing him. The time to fire a broadside had arrived. Time to vent everything that was pent up within her.

"Why are you doing this? To be with that cheap trashy girl? And her filthy urchin? To be someone's messenger boy for the rest of your life?"

Calm down. Be once again the girl that he kissed on the Common. Remember?

"Reef. You must believe me. I love you."

"I love Anita, Robin, and I don't want to miss that sparkle."

"The what?"

"That sparkle in her eyes."

"What are you talking about?"

"Her eyes. Her brilliant smile. Her laughter. I almost threw them away, didn't I?"

Robin was losing everything. Think of something. Crawl.

"Please. Don't leave me. Don't leave me. Get on board with me. Now."

"No."

No? I'm Robin Larimore. How dare you?

"I won't agree to a dissolution. Never."

Two long howls escaped from the steamer's whistle. Reef took his sea bag off the cart as the porter was returning. Sailors began slackening the lines, as he pushed Robin up the gangplank.

"It doesn't matter. I'm not staying in San Francisco. I have friends in Utah Territory. I'm taking Anita and J.J. with me."

Robin fired one last futile shot, shouting above the din of the departing ship.

"And when did you come up with that insane idea?"

"A couple of days ago. I packed a little girl into a trunk. She was on her way to Utah Territory."

"You did what? You're insane. Utah Territory is one flight up from hell. You'll never fit in with those people. Come with me, Reef. I demand that you get on board."

Reef's answer was not heard by Robin, or by anyone but himself.

"Goodbye, Robin."

"Damn you, Reef Atherton. You get on board this instant."

Reef returned to the dock and the gangplank was stowed. He watched the dockhands cast off the lines, he heard the propeller begin to turn, and he watched the ship ease away from the dock. He looked at Robin, ever so beautiful, bordering on God-kneeling perfection, standing there on the deck. He felt the remains of the dogtype in his coat pocket and removed it. He took one last look at the photograph, her dress, her hair, her eyes, and her lips. He dropped the photograph into the water and watched it sink, her image disappearing inch by inch, until it was out of sight.

"Goodbye, Robin," he whispered once more.

Reef had one more detail to attend. He turned and walked away from the water without looking back. Robin had tears in her eyes as she screamed his name again and again until it was drowned in the racket of the embarkation frenzy.

He was only human. He was mortal and vulnerable. He had risked his life for his little friend. He had succeeded and he had walked away untouched. Something seemed to smolder within him, and then it ignited, and breathed into him new warmth. A sense of flight inflated his soul, and he sensed that he was soaring.

He felt a sudden chill. Then, a thrill and a feeling of pleasure engulfed him. A surge pushed him and transcended him into heights of self-esteem and confidence. The same feeling that came over him after downing a few drinks. Many drinks. A feeling that he was drunk.

This time, though, he was not drunk. He had merely *won*. He had prevailed. He had bet it all, all that he was, all that he had, and he had triumphed. Let no one challenge him now, for he was invincible. He had conquered his fears and his limitations. He was free.

The feeling lasted a scant three or four minutes, followed by a depression that lasted thirty or forty, with its accompanying recriminations. He could have been killed. He should have been killed. He chose to shield a precious poke, this one not of fawnskin and filled with gold, but of cotton denim and filled with flesh and bone. A self-absorbed little creature known as a kid.

He had abandoned his primal instinct and sacred duty to save himself, to grope for his pistol and cover his corpus. The choice had been his, and with one motion, he had abdicated all responsibility to himself. This time, he had won. He had descended into hellfire, and fate and the gods above had resurrected him. He was well pleased with his choice and even more with the outcome.

And he was lonely. He could share this feeling with no one. This feeling was his alone. Now he was defined. Reef knew who he was, what he was, and what he had been seeking all along. Not the wealth and happiness that gold could bring him, or numbers of ships, or Boston's Beacon Hill.

He did not like poetry. But there was something from which he could not escape. Something having to do with missing someone. His held his sea bag high above him with his arm outstretched and let it crash down upon the porch. He opened the screen door, let it slam against the outside wall of the little ramshackle frame house, and announced himself.

"I missed you."

A few quick steps brought his body into contact with the little freckle-nosed girl doing the dishes in the midst of soap suds, tears, and a runny nose. He would allow no reprimand from her, no alarm, no protest, and above all no refusal.

Only submission. For now, he was purged of the wealthy Robin, the nightmares of chained Negroes, and the *Polar Star* and its Chinese sing-song girls. All that he wanted in life was here in his arms, and he would have her tonight.

"You once told me that a man loves the girl he misses. I forgot the rest, so you remind me. Who does a girl love? And you answer me right."

His proposal was cut short by her quick turn that brought the faces of the two lovers together, his with an intense and unyielding resolve, and hers with tears in her bright blue eyes, and a honey-sprinkled voice that alternated between laughter and sobbing.

"She will love the one she kisses."

She kissed him, waited until he responded, then parted from him to punish him for forgetting. Reef was not satisfied with such a fleeting kiss or with his punishment, so he drove home his point.

"Are we going to get married or not?"

He's not going to get off that easy.

"You haven't asked me yet."

Darn it. Oh, ask her. Go ahead, ask her.

"Will you?"

I want more than that. Make him say it.

"Will I what?"

Oh, all right. I give up.

"Marry me?"

That's it!

"Of course I will."

She kissed him again, this time letting him taste as much of her as he wanted.

"March 25, 1855 ... I made him spend that night in his room at the Barclay Hotel. And every night until our wedding. He pouted and he pleaded like a little boy. He did not like it one bit! (Neither did I.)

We marry today. I will make it all up to him tonight. Oh, I do love him so."

Diary of Anita Travis

Atherton